M000012528

contents

copyright

first edition

ISBN-13: 978-1-6720-9395-8

acknowledgements

thank You, God, for the beautiful, curious mystery of creation and for new mercy daily;

thank you to Jeremie Benzinger for the incredible cover art;

thank you to Rob Pettigrew, who read through large portions of the manuscript as i was doing final edits and formatting to publish, giving lots of guidance on proper terminology and military protocol (some of which i ignored, so don't blame him for that);

thank you to Ret. Brigadier General Karen Rizzuti; Ron Carlson; Clark Wakham; Pat Steffans; the research staff at Penrose Library in Colorado Springs, especially Mariah Hudson, Toni Miller, Tim Morris, and volunteers like J. Richards; and the Peterson Air Force Base Museum, especially Gail Whalen; and Dick Burns; all for their valuable insights into military life and protocol, planes, the United States Air Force, the CONAD Command Center, military history, life in Colorado Springs, and other things i knew nothing about when i started writing this story;

thank you to Donut Country and Starbucks (Fortress, Memorial, and Keith & 1st) who gave me space to create, immeasurable kindness, and also coffee and donuts;

thank you to ninjas for being ninjas, without whose encouragement and wisdom i could not have completed this project;

thank you to all of my friends and family who have encouraged this and other projects along the way;

thank you to everyone who has served to protect this country and free others from forces that would keep men, women, and children in bondage, poverty, darkness, and injustice;

and thank you to mom and dad for always, always believing in me.

introduction

this was supposed to be a short story i could whip out quickly. i was compiling several ideas to fill out a short story collection i could release as a paperback, along with "kindling", "the darkness rolled over her", and "ciao bella". i'd had this idea for a few years as a possible short film, but hadn't even done much mental work on it yet. i figured i could quickly construct a fun Christmas story and move on to other projects.

once i started diving into the history, a story began emerging that i chased through many months of research, phone calls, location visits, declassified PDFs, technical manuals, newspaper clippings, outlines, rewrites upon rewrites, and lots of unexpected soul searching.

the result is the novel you hold in your hand. i wanted so badly to spend more months re-writing, but i wanted to publish in time for Christmas. even so, i am very happy with the finished product.

i hope God Rest Ye Merry Gentlemen takes you on a range of emotions, keeps you turning pages, and invites you to share it with someone else.

*but mostly i hope it helps you appreciate peace on earth —
where it exists — and prompts you to ask yourself what cost you're
willing to endure so peace on earth may flourish.*

Godspeed.

God Rest Ye Merry Gentlemen

"...having made peace through the blood of his cross, by Him to reconcile all things unto Himself; by Him, I say, whether they be things in earth, or things in heaven."
— *Colossians 1:20, KJV*

"the word reconcile *shows the enmity; the words* having made peace, *the war."*
— *John Chrysostom, homily on Colossians 1:20*

prologue

the following story is based on real events that occurred December 1955. some of the details are public knowledge, a matter of public record, and historically verifiable.

other details have never been presented to the public, until now. according to the United States Air Force, Army, Joint Chiefs of Staff, NORAD, the Pentagon, Congress, the White House, and former officials from the Union of Soviet Socialist Republics, these portions of the story never happened.

but to properly honor the actions of Clarence Todd and Kenneth Abernathy (and men and women like them), the story is presented here, in full, with no redactions.

silent night

David scowled as his fellow airman emptied a flask of whiskey into the punch bowl.

"wipe that sourpuss off your face, Michaels. it's just a little Christmas cheer."

"you're not even old enough to drink liquor."

"i'll be 21 in a couple of months."

"in a couple of months." if one thing had been instilled in Airman First Class David Michaels over the past year and a half, it was respect for the letter of the law. somehow Howard Alspach had made it to the same rank with a slightly looser interpretation.

"are you telling me," Howard said as he poured, "you've never had liquor?"

David squirmed. "well. i had some of my uncle's moonshine when i was 5. i thought it was water."

"see? same thing." Howard stirred the punch bowl with the ladle, playing with the frozen sherbet bobbing about the middle. "don't be such a square."

"i'm not a square," David said, fiddling with a button on the cuff of his uniform. "i just don't like what it does to people."

"well," Howard said. "you don't have to have any." Howard turned to the sink and rinsed the flask.

David stared at the bowls of nuts and candies on the break room table. this was not the Christmas he wanted. it was his first Christmas away from home, away from mom and dad. he wanted to be at his grandparents' house, sitting by the radiator, watching Perry Como or Lawrence Welk. or at the farm, a huge bonfire roaring in front of the cabin, listening to Uncle P.B.'s stories. anywhere the dimly-lit warmth of home could spark those mysterious feelings he loved most about Christmas. it was hard to feel Christmas-y in full uniform under the fluorescent lights of the Continental Air Defense Combat Operations Center breakroom. the hard, white tiles under his freshly polished loafers were cold to look at.

Howard stuck a paper cup full of tap water in front of David's face. "look at it this way. at least you're getting paid to be here." Howard was kind of a jerk sometimes, but he'd always been a decent friend. "it really is water, i promise."

"i'm fine," David said, taking the cup. "i enlisted to serve any time. it's just..."

"you wanted to be behind an instrument panel, not a tanker desk?"

"yeah."

Howard set his large frame into the chair next to David. "the military lives and dies on paperwork, champ."

"i'm not saying it's not important. i'd just rather be home with my family at Christmas."

"we all would."

"but you're from here."

"yeah. i'll have lunch with mom and dad tomorrow. but we do gifts on Christmas Eve. so i'll miss that."

"they can't wait?"

"i'm the oldest of nine, so, no."

"nine. good grief."

"yyyup."

"well at least you get to go home."

"what, you can't make it to Kentucky and back before shift tomorrow?"

David chuckled. "my desk only does 200 miles an hour. it'd be a tight turnaround."

Howard laughed.

"it's just going to be so boring tonight."

"you better hope it's boring."

"i meant-- well, yes. i know what you mean. i just want to be making some progress against the enemy."

"the Russians have their head up their ass. we're years beyond them in terms of airpower, organization, funding, i mean... you name it. they don't even have aircraft carriers."

"i heard they just finished a big bomb."

"ours are bigger. anyway, they've had big bombs."

"no, this is a real, thermonuclear bomb. maybe as large as three megatons."

"don't believe that baloney. Soviet propaganda." Howard ladled some of the red punch into a cup. "besides, how they gonna get it here? put it on a boat?"

"their bombers can reach our coasts."

"and we have early warning detection on the coasts. you think their bombers are invisible?"

"i don't know. who knows what they're doing."

"don't spend your life paranoid, sport." Howard thunked his big feet into the chair next to him and leaned back, relaxed. "the good ol' USA has something the Ruskies don't."

"what's that?"

Howard winked and held out his cup. "us."

David smiled and touched his cup to Howard's.

"cheers, mate."

"you two celebrating already?" the relative silence of the break room disappeared as George Gordy and Leonard Cesana clamored in. Gordy pulled a flask from his small duffel bag. Howard let out a halting grunt.

"i already spiked it."

Gordy paused, then kept unscrewing the lid. "ah, a little more won't kill us."

Howard rose and pushed the flask back away from the bowl. "we're on duty, Gordy. save it for new year's."

Leonard opened and slammed counter doors, searching. "where's the nosh?"

Howard plucked a candied almond from one of the dishes and beaned Leonard in the back of the head with it. "it's on the table, moron."

"what, this? i thought we were gonna have a spread. some pastrami, prosciutto, something."

"it's in the fridge."

Leonard opened the fridge and stuck his head in, peering around the Coca-Cola bottles and leftover lunches. he leaned so far in, David thought he might actually crawl inside it. Leonard was from New York and wasn't satisfied with his food unless it was accompanied by any number of salty pork meats. Gordy kept trying to push around Howard with the flask. even though Howard was tall and solid, Gordy had the mass (width) to push him out of the way, but everybody respected Howard. he'd be a Senior Airman before any of the rest of them, and everyone knew it.

giving up, Gordy turned to the television on the counter and started clunking through channels and fiddling with the antenna.

"reception is shit in here." Gordy was able to get a staticky feed of Roy Rogers to come into focus.

"turn this kid's stuff," Leonard barked. *kid's stuff?*, David thought. David loved Roy Rogers.

Gordy shoved Leonard in the sternum. "give me a second, will ya, i'm workin on it." the channel knob thunked from station to station — *I Love Lucy*, opera, the Saturday Matinee.

"wrestling starts at four," Leonard grunted, rubbing his chest.

"wrestling was at two." Gordy retorted.

"wrestling starts at four!"

"your shift starts at four, knuckleheads." but they both gave Howard a dismissive wave.

"i'm going to go get my station ready," David said, rising.

Howard followed him to the door. "Michaels. it's saturday night, it's Christmas Eve... try to relax tonight. okay?" over Howard's shoulder, David watched Gordy empty his flask into the punch bowl.

"yeah, okay," David nodded and headed to his cubicle.

relaxing wasn't the issue. it's true, he'd not had a full day off since Thanksgiving, and that was only two days. it wasn't enough time for him to travel home even if he'd had a car, which he didn't.

there was usually nothing strenuous to do, unless they were running drills. they had just finished their largest drill ever a couple of weeks ago, Operation Crackerjack. it was a simulation of a massive Soviet air attack and the first fully-operational demonstration of Continental Air Defense as the hub for all communications during such an attack. it came as a surprise early in David's shift on a Monday and lasted about 13 hours, with most everyone involved with the Command Center involved in some way. overall, the exercise was a mixed bag. some things went right, and some short-comings were revealed, which they'd already started working on. during the drill, everyone was working at full speed, long hours, barking and taking orders, and consulting their myriad manuals for how to respond to the various scenarios presented by the drill. the Pentagon had seemed happy with it, but a lot of the directives that had been handed down in the ensuing days made it clear: there was a lot of room for improvement. it made David proud to have been part of such a massive system put in place to protect so many people, but he wondered if it really would.

when the drill was over, there was massive data gathering. the Colonels and Majors went over everything again and again, replaying individual moments ad nauseam. top brass had been granted some r&r for the holidays, but most of the grunts were left cross-referencing the data — maps, flight trajectories, response times. all of this data was cataloged, copied, and cross-referenced by David and his fellow airmen in their cubicles deep in the "den" hidden below the tiered Command Center theater. while important Air Force and Army stars sat high up looking at wall-sized maps, the airmen toiled below. during the drill, there was lots of activity — running radios, updating maps with the latest info, communicating by phone with bases in California, Alaska, and New Jersey. but after the drill, it was all paperwork, and lots of it.

and David found himself bored. he kept reminding himself that paperwork and all the more tedious aspects of his job were just as important. that would usually help him get through the day.

but not today. not on Christmas Eve. not when he wanted to be at home with his family. not when his fellow airmen were making it clear they had little intention of getting anything done. no, tonight they were just holding down the fort.

as David stepped out of the break room and into the front lobby, the last of the morning shift crew was wrapping up and heading home. stairwells on either side of the lobby led to the upper tiers of the Command Center. David pushed through the double doors in the center, entering the tunnel that divided the dens from the conference room. the lights at the end of the tunnel came mostly from the large maps on the wall in front of him, huge plexiglass maps with grease pencil markings all over. a first-shift airman cleaned one as David stepped out into the pit, the open floor at the base of the theater. he looked up at the two tiers of phones, desk lamps, ashtrays, and manila folders. important men wrapped up their business for the day, and they seemed to be happy about going home. David sighed.

the Colonel was still at his desk in the big glass cab atop the theater. surely he had plans to spend Christmas Eve and Morning with his family. but he sipped coffee as he stood over his desk, flipping through large drafting schematics of who-knows-what. was he avoiding his family? surely not. *although, not all families are like mine*, David reminded himself. he added that sadness to his own disappointment as he dipped back out of the bright theater and into the den.

David's first-shift counterpart happily turned over some logs they shared and got him up to speed on their progress. most of it was preparation for a very detailed debrief on Operation Crackerjack after the first of the new year. David sighed, taking the giant binders into his possession. he hoped they would be crucial data that moved the CONAD program forward, but in his heart he knew they'd likely be the umpteenth appendix in a document no one would read anyway. the first shift crew left as quickly as they were allowed, and with Gordy, Leonard, Howard, and the others still in the break room, David sat alone in the dim, silent den.

after he wiped the dust off everything on his desk, he checked to make sure his stapler was full.

it was.

it was going to be a long night.

§

the most wonderful time of the year

eventually, the other airmen wound their way through the catacombs of cubicles, laughing and chattering loudly, lips and cheeks red from punch. Gordy and Leonard climbed onto nearby filing cabinets to hang a Merry Christmas banner from the drop ceiling. Howard watched from a safe distance, holding the paper cup full of "Christmas cheer", decorated with designs of holly leaves and berries around the rim. in the corner, someone had set up a small aluminum Christmas tree, the multicolored cellophane wheel spinning slowly in front of the lamp underneath. it wasn't home, but it was Christmas. and he was with friends. he'd try to enjoy what he could of it.

a smattering of applause and cheers broke out as Mo entered, holding a portable turntable with a wooden crate of LPs and 45s on top. 'Mo' was actually Technical Sergeant Bernard Bonner. during basic military training, his name was shortened to 'B.B.', which led to 'Bravo Bravo', which led to 'Bravissimo', which had been shortened to just 'Mo', and that one seemed to take. Howard slapped Mo on the back as he laid his load onto a tanker desk that wasn't his.

"whatcha got for us tonight, my friend?"

"a buddy of mine sent me a new song he just recorded. you guys gotta hear it. it's like country, but, rock. i dunno. it's new."

"Sarge, ain't ya got any Christmas songs?" David asked.

"i got Christmas songs, Michaels. don't get your panties in a wad."

"my panties?"

Howard leaned in, "we're gonna be here for eight hours tonight. relax."

"i'm relaxed." David hated being spoken to like a child. he never understood why people treated him like a child just because he didn't want to engage in the same raucous behaviors they did.

Gordy shoved a cracker into a hamball he held on a plate. "hey i thought Pepper was the only Sergeant here tonight." Dan 'Pepper' Donaldson earned his nickname from his already-graying hair, even though he was a hale twenty-five years old. he was tall and thin, capable and kind. Pepper always came and sat with David in the break room on meal breaks. David liked him. David didn't dislike Mo, but did find him to be rude and brash, qualities that often made tense situations worse.

Mo responded. "uh, Pepper, yes, was technically supposed to be the only Tech Sergeant on duty. i've been assigned a bit of... a... behavioral--"

"ah yes ah technically ah the only ah a bit," Leonard mocked. "Colonel gave you bitch duty for mouthing off to him during handoff yesterday."

"get bent, Lenny. nobody likes you."

"your mothah likes me!" Leonard laughed as he thumbed through the albums. Mo swiped them out of his hands and put them back into a neat stack.

"i got these in order."

"Gordy get that funky hamball back in the break room." everyone turned to see Lieutenant Colonel James Boyd entering, raincoat over his arm, briefcase in hand.

"ah, c'mon, sir. can't we have some snacks in the work room tonight? it's Christmas."

"it's Christmas *Eve*, and i don't care if you eat in here, but no one wants smell your funky hamball all night."

"my girl made it."

"did she slaughter one of her own?" Mo asked.

"call my girlfriend a pig one more time and see if i don't give you a fat lip."

"yeah, well, you know from fat lips, for sure."

Gordy rushed at him as Howard jumped in between them. "settle down, Gordy, he's just pushing your buttons."

"Gordy!" Boyd barked.

"yes sir?"

"hamball. out."

"yes, sir."

"i think that's how he asks his girl on a date," Mo whispered.

"keep it up, Mo!" Gordy yelled from the tunnel. David followed him.

"where you going, Michaels?" Boyd asked.

"well, sir, i kinda wanted some of that hamball."

"trust me, you don't. i had one bite of it last year, gave me the runs for a week. listen, grab your logs and bring them to the conference room. i want to go over a few of those issues we ran into during the drill."

"yes, Lieutenant Colonel." David walked back to his station, his stomach growling. hamball or not, he was going to need to eat a little something soon. he'd had a quick sandwich at home for breakfast, but that wasn't going to last him for eight hours. he should have planned better.

he gathered up some paperwork and his pouch of measuring instruments. slid into the manuals under the hutch of his desk was his big, black Bible. he pulled it out and flipped through it, landing on Luke 2. he pulled the ribbon down into the crease between the thin pages. maybe he'd have a chance to read the Christmas story to everyone tonight. some of these guys needed some Jesus.

a commotion erupted as Mo knocked over a rolling chair. he steadied himself, standing on the desk. "it's fine. i'm fine." he lifted a speaker from the wall and disconnected the wires from behind it. he hopped down off the desk, righted the chair, then used it as a makeshift cart for his records, turntable, and the speaker, and started wheeling it off toward the pit.

"wha-- he can't take that, can he?"

everyone looked at David, annoyed. Howard approached him with that 'big brother' look on his face.

"what do we need the PA for? there's like seven us, and we're all in here."

David frowned. he slapped his Bible shut and shoved it in his binder.

David flipped the switch and the fluorescent lights flickered to life over the conference room table. it was a large room, designed to hold about twenty people, the chief personnel needed during an attack. it had three windowless walls, and its interior wall along the tunnel was all glass, which had earned it the nickname 'the fishbowl'. tonight, it felt even smaller than usual. the long, grey conference table looked like one of those stainless steel tables in a morgue, occasionally dotted with notepads and ashtrays. David set

14

his giant binder down with a thud. electronic screeching could be heard from the workroom as the guys fiddled with the turntable.

Lieutenant Colonel Boyd came in carrying his own binders and a couple of maps rolled up and tucked under his arm. he walked to the far end of the table and set everything down.

"scoot this way and make room for Walter." David admired Walter. Boyd loved 2nd Lieutenant Walter Gamble like a little brother, and Walter greatly respected Boyd. everyone liked having them directly over them. they were easy-going and hard-working. David especially liked them because they were the only two to treat him like a capable adult. Walter treated him as a peer, and Boyd respected David as a capable airman. the only downside to being in Boyd's squad was that meant working on Christmas Eve this year.

"Walter needs half the table?" David slid his heavy notebook down the formica tabletop as he walked.

"he does." Boyd dropped into a rolling chair, pulled himself to the table, and began unrolling maps.

"how'd you end up with the Christmas overnight shift, sir?"

Boyd smiled, keeping a secret. "i... made my opinion known during the Crackerjack drill."

"when you called the Colonel a hothead, sir?"

Boyd's smile disappeared along with his secret. "grab a pen, Michaels."

"yessir." David grabbed a pad and pen and sat down.

"tonight, we are using these charts of the Atlantic and verifying ranges of attack based on known Soviet aircraft and known Soviet air bases. we'll cross reference the maps with your logs on the DEW line ranges, see what gaps remain, and offer up a proposal for connecting the West Coast line with the East Coast..."

David nodded, making notes as Boyd went on about the plan for the night. *very festive*, David thought. music began to drift in from the pit, meaning they'd gotten the turntable working. it seemed like it might be the only thing they'd accomplish all night.

the twangy music cut into the room as the door opened. Second Lieutenant Walter Gamble pushed through a cart loaded with tinfoil-wrapped roast pots and ceramic dinnerware. Walter was slim and fit with round spectacles. because of his humility you'd never know it, but he was fast and strong. he'd be the strongest of the crew if he weren't but 130 pounds, and was as smart as he was agile. Walter was just all around a good man. the only reason not to like him was there was no reason not to like him. Walter began setting out dishes onto the table.

"better fix you a plate before the rest of them get a whiff," Boyd said without looking up.

"thank you, sir." David rose and walked toward the feast.

"fix me one, too, will ya?"

Walter removed the tin foil from the first platter and the smell of warm smoked turkey filled the room.

"that smells amazing," David said.

"we've also got pizza from Giuseppe's and ice cream from Michelle's."

David helped him get everything on the table. there was a pot roast with onion, carrots, and big chunks of potato. chicken casserole, green beans, creamed spinach, potato salad, three different Jell-Os, and a strawberry cake for dessert. there was enough food to feed 30 people, and then some.

"thank you for dinner, sir," David said.

"told you to skip the hamball."

"yessir."

Boyd watched out for David. David didn't usually like the special attention; it embarrassed him. the others seems to resent him for it. but right now he was thankful to get first crack at everything. David piled a plate high with a little bit of everything, then walked it to Lt. Col. Boyd.

"here you go, sir."

Boyd smiled, then looked out the glass wall across the tunnel. "better hurry."

David and Walter grabbed plates for themselves as Gordy stepped through the fishbowl door, hypnotically drawn by the aroma that had passed through the lobby.

§

do you hear what i hear

soon the conference room was full with nearly everyone on duty that night. David sat at the working end of the table with Walter and Boyd, careful not to drop any cranberry sauce on his charts. Walter and Boyd chatted, and David read his Bible while he ate.

Gordy and Leonard sat next to them, arguing if corn or tomatoes made a better side.

"corn's not a vegetable, even," Leonard said, fully aware Gordy was born and raised on a Nebraska farm.

"say that again," Gordy threatened, an elephant ear of ham flapping from the tines of the fork he jabbed at Leonard.

"it's a grain. besides tomatoes go with everything."

"tomatoes are a fruit."

"you take that back!" Leonard barked, lobbing a chunk of fresh mozzarella into Gordy's tie.

behind them, the three youngest airmen, Dickie Marston, Bill Sollee, and Joey Burke sat on the floor, paper plates in their laps, just thankful for hot food that wasn't from the mess hall. David only had about a year on them, but it felt like a decade. they looked like boys. David didn't feel like a boy any more.

Mo entered, loudly. "i'm taking requests. dollar a play."

"dollar?" Leonard shouted back. "c'mon, the jukebox is three songs for a quarter!"

"go find you a jukebox then." Mo leaned over David and snatched up his Bible.

"hey!" David protested.

"you need to get your nose outta that book, Michaels. have some punch. maybe you'll lighten up for a change."

David glanced at Boyd, who was still talking with Walter, oblivious. David wanted to yell back, but Mo was a Technical Sergeant, his superior. while they often talked casually while working, David didn't want to have an argument with him in front of everyone. Mo tossed the Bible into the center of the table between the neapolitan and the rocky road and sat down at the other end.

immediately, Mo started prattling on about his buddy's new record as Pepper ate next to him in silence, listening, or pretending to. *the man has the patience of Job*, David thought. Pepper had tried to find a spot near David, but others had gotten their first. David wasn't sure why Pepper seemed to enjoy eating with him. maybe it was just to stay away from Mo.

1st Lieutenant Benji Demonbruen walked in, leaned over Mo, and grabbed a roll from Mo's plate. no one could pronounce Demonbruen, despite Benji's explanation it was just French for "from Brown Mountain". all anybody heard was "French", and so he was called Froggy. and once you had a nickname, it stuck. Froggy popped the roll into Mo's open mouth.

Mo yanked it and glared up at his superior. "i'm not hungry, sir," he said with as little respect as possible.

"yeah, i know, but we're tired of listening to you." everyone laughed but Mo. even David.

"as you were," boomed a voice from the open door, dripping with irony. everyone was so caught up in eating, they'd not noticed the brass at the door — Majors Ed McKellar and John Tilday. Burke, Sollee, and Marston fumbled all over, dropping food, trying to stand.

Boyd stayed them with a hand, "he said 'as you were', airmen. relax. sit. eat."

"yessir," the trio said in unison. and they sat, trying to reassemble their plates.

"you can command them to sit, but you can't command them to relax," Walter whispered to David, chuckling.

the Majors pushed through the seated bodies toward the food. Major McKellar was strict and formal, the perfect military man. he had been Army air before the declaration of a separate Air Force. he was an experienced veteran, a talented pilot, and all soldier. David thought it strange to see this respected authority piling mashed potatoes onto a paper plate, as if he never ate or did things that normal people did. David had these same thoughts whenever Major McKellar came to chapel or devotional times at the base. fraternizing wasn't allowed, but in chapel, everyone is equal, and Major McKellar was just Ed. there, David learned Ed was really into cars. he had a few roadsters from the 20s, and he liked to drag race. get him talking about one of his roadsters, and his eyes would sparkle, and he'd smile and laugh. but then back at the Command Center, he was Major McKellar. Major McKellar never sparkled or smiled. it was hard for David to see Ed and Major McKellar as the same person.

David didn't really know Major Tilday, but he liked him. he was kind and quiet and had been a medic during the War. the

Majors each fixed two plates, presumably for Captains Freeman and Milton still up in the cab. a capable officer squad always needed to be on alert. even during a makeshift Christmas dinner, someone important had to be watching the phone.

"someone bring a plate up for the Colonel, will ya?" Major Tilday said. and with plates piled high, the Majors went back up to the cab.

Gordy stood up. "i got it." Gordy was not one to volunteer for anything, but he mowed the Colonel's yard, so he felt neighborly with him.

Sollee slapped Burke in the chest to get his attention, and again, like three blind mice, the young airmen scrambled to stand. at the door was Major Pete Roberts.

"as you were," Major Roberts said, surveying the room — people first, then the food. "except you, Bonner. i could hear you from the tiers." and Roberts shoved a roll in his mouth, inciting another round of laughs. Roberts had a sarcastic way about him that a lot of the guys took for melancholy, but David thought he was funny, which made him feel like he was in on the joke. still, he was an officer, and a stoic, and the airmen kept their distance from him. and he returned the favor. done constructing his plate, he slipped back into the tunnel without a word.

and within a few minutes there was a lull in the room. everyone's mouth was full.

"did anyone say a blessing?" a lot of mixed reactions spun David's way.

"you can say your own," Mo said.

"i was eating with gratitude," Howard said, which prompted a few chuckles.

"great idea, Mo," said Lt. Col. Boyd, standing. everyone nervously sat their plates down and stood with him. everyone but

Mo. Boyd looked at David. "why don't you say your own blessing, loud enough for the rest of us to feel blessed as well."

David swallowed hard. one of Boyd's chief operating principles was, if you're complaining, you're volunteering to head up the solution.

Mo rolled his eyes and stood with everyone else. all eyes were on David. this wasn't a prayer. it was David's prayer. and now David's prayer was just interrupting everyone's meal.

David cleared his throat. "please bow your heads." the room became silent, motionless. "give us grateful hearts, our Father, for all Thy mercies, and make us mindful of the needs of others; through Jesus Christ our Lord. amen."

a chorus of amens, Leonard crossed himself, and Howard patted David on the shoulder. an "at ease" from Boyd, and everyone was back chatting and eating again.

David sat and picked at his food, embarrassed. he could feel Walter looking at him, which made him more embarrassed. he didn't like being pitied. or patted. it was that whole being-treated-like-a-child thing.

"what's on your mind, Michaels," Walter asked.

most of what was on his mind he didn't care to share with Walter. so he just skimmed the surface. "missin Christmas dinner with my family."

"with this spread?"

"oh this is great. it's just different. we'd have salted ham, corn, chicken stew, sweet potatoes. cornbread and pinto beans. pecan pie with hot butter--"

"golly, Michaels. i thought y'all were dirt poor," Leonard said. "what'd you rob a casino or something?"

"no. we had a farm. meat, eggs, milk, fruits and veggies — we had all that. we didn't have peanut butter. or bread sometimes."

"yah didn't have bread?"

"store-bought stuff was hard to come by. i never had a Oreo til basic."

"i never had a steak before the mess hall," Marston said from the floor behind them.

"got news for ya, Dickie." Howard nudged him with his foot. "you still haven't." Howard whinnied loudly, cracking an imaginary whip, and the other airmen laughed.

"try Christmas in a New York apartment," Leonard said. "we were lucky to afford a tree."

"BUY a Christmas tree?" David said. "good law, who on earth would pay for a Christmas tree?"

"where'd you get your tree?"

"backyard."

"we don't got backyards in Brooklyn, Michaels."

"if it's any consolation, Michaels," said Mo, "we all wish you were back home, too." Howard burned a look Mo's direction, but Mo was forking his next bite of pie. David wasn't ever surprised when Mo lashed out, but there was an awkwardness hanging in the room, and David was the focus of it. and he just wanted it to end.

Leonard, oblivious, continued. "one thing we did have is snow."

"we get lots of snow here," Howard said, like Leonard was stupid.

"on Christmas," Leonard said. "it was 70-somethin today."

"we don't get a lot of snow in Southern Kentucky. i haven't had a white Christmas since i was 13. i thought surely i'd have one here."

"snow is overrated," Howard said.

"it's pretty," David said.

"pretty?" said Leonard.

David's face flashed red, which he hoped no one could see. "to look at."

"for a few minutes maybe," Howard said. "after you're done feeding the cows, the frozen mud is just a big mess."

David thanked God when Gordy clamored through the door. "you guys see about this storm last night?" he plopped into his chair and went right back to eating. in his free hand was a folded up newspaper.

"it shook the whole barracks, Gordy," Howard said. "it was kinda hard to miss."

"i heard it ripped up Pike's Peak pretty bad. like tornadoes or somethin," Leonard said.

Burke spoke up. "it was straightline winds."

Leonard spun around to see who spoke. it wasn't often anyone heard Burke say a word. "what're straightline winds?"

"exactly what it sounds like," Burke said. David chuckled, and Leonard shot him a dirty look.

Gordy tapped the newspaper with a finger. "power's still out on the Peak," he continued, as Pepper looked at the article, perhaps as an excuse to not have to listen to Mo any more. "and paper says it busted out plate glass windows and snapped phone lines downtown. tore down a bunch of those hand-made Christmas decorations."

"Mr. Noxon won't be happy about that," Howard said. David felt like such a foreigner in every way. he was a little jealous that Howard got to serve here in his own hometown.

Boyd rose from the head of the conference room table. "fifteen minutes, men. then be back at your posts. Michaels, Gamble, you're here with me going over these reports."

"yessir," Walter and David said.

Boyd put some cookies on a clean plate and left the fishbowl. David pushed his plate aside and started looking at his charts, his mind elsewhere.

Howard sat down where Boyd had been. in his hand was David's Bible. "i'm glad you're here."

"thanks." David took the Bible from him and tucked it back into his binder. he appreciated the gesture, but it just felt patronizing.

"do you enjoy being here?" Howard asked.

he didn't. he didn't join the Air Force for fun, but he thought there would be some kind of joy, fulfillment, something like that. and there was. in small ways, from time to time. but to constantly feel like a stranger among the very people who are supposed to be your brothers-in-arms... David believed a joy should be there that wasn't there. there should be peace, but instead, he was anxious. David realized he hadn't answered yet, which he figured was enough of an answer for Howard. "why did you join the Air Force?" David asked Howard.

"because planes are *bitchin.*"

David sat up. "what do you mean?"

"our farm outside of town shared a border with this huge junkyard, we're talking hundreds of cars, big haulin trucks, farm equipment. Larry, the guy that owned it, he was this old, Texas redneck. his grandson and i worked at BJ's together. anyway, Larry had this TBM Avenger he'd bought at an auction, after the Air Force realized they were too slow to be a fighter and too small to be a bomber. well, they put in this little dirt runway, and he converted the bomb bay to hold a few hundred pounds of dirt and manure—"

"manure?" Walter said, leaning forward.

"cow shit."

"i know what manure is."

"he'd buy it from us cheap. we were literally up to our knees in it with the cattle farm, and it saved us the trouble of bagging it up and taking it to market for fertilizer or something. since we were next door it was literally cheaper than dirt, like, going and buying a truckload of dirt somewhere."

"but why manure in the plane?" Walter asked, getting Howard back on topic.

"they constantly had these tire fires in a back corner of the junkyard. we're talking thousands of tires. and once a tire fire starts, you can smell it and see it for miles. he'd wind that plane up and do flyovers past the tire fires. and he'd dump that manure across it to put it out."

the other men around them had stopped eating and were listening to Howard's yarn.

"but, wait, isn't manure flammable?" Gordy asked.

"not by the truckload-full. dump it on a rubber fire and it snuffs right out. and i mean, it was a sight. just a wall of shit hanging in the air. and when it fell, he could land that pile within inches of where he wanted it. i even saw him do it in high wind one time — incredible. he was an expert pilot. and that was inspiring. but mainly, it was just the plane. it was cool as hell. had the ball turret and everything. he used it to help us find a lost calf on our property once. and when he found it, he just kept circling until we were able to chase it down. i remember riding in the back of my dad's pickup with a lasso, that ornery little t-bone loping across the pasture at full sprint, and that Avenger was going back and forth right over us, tracking with us, going as slow as he could, in case the calf got away from us. i was supposed to be watching the calf, but.. i couldn't keep my eyes off that plane."

the room was rapt.

"not surprised your hero is full of shit," Mo said, and the room erupted. it even made David laugh, though David didn't like that kind of language.

"kiss my ass, Mo," Howard said, tossing a roll at Mo from across the room. "why are you in the Air Force?"

"who, me?" Mo asked.

"yes, you."

"i just do it to get women."

everyone laughed.

"my dad was in the Army Air Corp," Leonard said. "so it was either Air Force or get disowned."

"well, Lenny," Howard said. "i think i speak for the others when i say, i wish he'd disowned you."

everyone laughed again. Leonard shot him a finger, laughing.

"what about you, Michaels?"

David had forgotten Howard's elaborate — no doubt embellished — story had begun as an answer to David's question. and now it had been turned back on him, and everyone looked at him, waiting for his answer.

"why'd you join the Air Force?" Howard asked.

David didn't have a prepared answer for this. it wasn't a clear moment in time like it was for Howard. and it had a lot to do with genuinely wanting to defend his country, and the American people, and a lot of other answers that made him sound more like he was running for office rather than a real person. his mouth dried, open.

Howard raised an eyebrow, waiting.

suddenly, out in the pit, the clatter of a loud bell arose, startling everyone. the only time they'd ever heard this bell was during drills, but there was no drill scheduled for tonight. David stood, frightened, before filing out of the fishbowl with the others into the open stadium of the Command Center.

the pit flashed red as a spinning light above the cab painted the large room. looking up across the tiers into the cab, David could see the brass were all sternly staring at the source of the alarm.

it was the red phone.

§

what child is this

everyone stood, frozen, for a split second that felt like an hour. the stillness shattered as Froggy bounded up the theater stairs and into the cab. everyone else stayed corralled on the pit floor. Major Roberts peeked out of the cab door as Froggy slipped through.

"Michaels," Roberts said calmly.

"yes, sir," David responded, as his face flushed, a mix of fear and anxiety, again being called out in front of the others.

"Pepper, Burke, Gamble." he waved a hand. the four young men walked to the staircase. the Major held the door open at the top of the stairs, letting them pass by him into the cab.

"Michaels," Roberts stopped David.

"get your book." David's face reddened again as he realized the other three had their binders and charts with them. David hustled back toward the fishbowl to get his binder. his hard heels on the metal stairs accentuated his aloofness. he grabbed his binder and a pencil and hot-footed it back up the stairs, watching his steps. he glanced at Mo as he passed him on the lower tier. he expected a judgmental 'get it together' from him, but Mo's gaze was locked on the booth. the ringing alarm stopped, but the red light kept flashing red across everyone in the Command Center. at the top of the stairs, Major Roberts put a hand on David's chest, stopping him.

"breathe, Michaels." David closed his eyes and took in a deep breath. he opened his eyes and Roberts nodded and let him pass. "everyone take five deep breaths," he called out to the stadium, and let the door close behind him.

the glass cab felt small and tight, like a tiny motel room. David was instantly hot, and the thick scent of cigarettes shallowed the air.

the Colonel was on the phone, raincoat draped over his arm, the Majors standing around him. David studied their faces for a clue. what would ring this phone? outside the Colonel and his boss, General Partridge, the only people who had the number to this phone were people high up at Strategic Air Command in Omaha, or the Pentagon, or the White House. the Colonel draped his coat over a chair. he appeared to be trying to decipher what he was hearing. not a good sign. the Majors were stoic, and seemed to be trying to decipher the Colonel's facial expressions the same as David. his stomach rolled over, and his skin clammed. the Colonel pulled the receiver away from his mouth and covered it with his hand.

"is this a joke?"

everyone in the room was stunned.

"is someone fooling around on the phones?"

"no, sir," Boyd responded. "what's happening?"

"this isn't that idiot Bonner? doesn't he work external communications?"

"yes, sir, but he's accounted for," Roberts reported. David looked down at the lower tier. Mo still stared into the glass. he and David locked eyes. David shrugged, no answers for him yet.

"what's happening, sir?" Boyd asked.

"it's some kid with his Christmas list." he flipped the switch for the speaker and hung up the hand set.

"... a Tonka truck, a Buck Rogers gun, and a J.C. Higgins bicycle."

the Colonel's look of confusion spread across everyone in the room, from the Majors to the Captains and on down the ranks. the speaker went silent, except for the young boy's breathing.

"hello?" the boy asked.

"son, how did you get this number?"

"maybe it's a wrong number," Roberts whispered.

"mommy dialed it."

more silence. everyone in the room was trying to come up with something, but at a loss.

"you're not the real Santa Claus."

the Colonel stared at the speaker.

everyone held their breath.

"ho ho ho!" the Colonel shouted. Roberts remained pokerfaced. Boyd's eyes got so big, David thought they might pop. a couple of men on the top tier heard through the glass and looked stunned. David didn't know what to make of any of this. if it was some holiday prank, it wasn't very funny. "i certainly am Santa Claus. have you been a good boy?"

"yes sir," the little voice said, with the sound of shuffling papers. "i have my sister's list, too. she wants a Tiny Tears doll and the Annie Oakley guns..."

"what is happening," Major Roberts said, mostly to himself, shaking his head. the Colonel listened to the young boy.

"and Santa, will you bring something nice for my mummy? she's been real good to me."

"what does she want, son."

"um. a pitcher for her Jewell Tea set."

"i think that's swell. is your mummy there?"

"yes."

"can i speak to her please?"

"yes."

"great. now you go get ready for bed. i can't stop by your house until you're asleep."

"okay. here's mummy."

"thank you, son. merry Christmas."

"merry Christmas."

the speaker clamored with the exchange, and an adult woman spoke. "hello?"

"ma'am, how did your son get this number?"

"the ad in the paper."

the men in the cab looked at each other. "ad?"

"in the evening Telegraph. is this... is this not the Santa hotline?"

Pepper quickly slipped out of the booth.

"no ma'am, it isn't," the Colonel said. "it's actually a classified line within the United States Armed Forces."

"oh my! oh i am so sorry... i must.. did i misdial?"

"well, that's what i'm trying to find out--"

"--i am so sorry, sir. please forgive me, sir."

"it's all right, no harm done, but i'd like to know if you misdialed or not. do you have that newspaper?"

"Ronnie," she whispered, "go in the kitchen and bring me the paper! yes, sir, we have it." rustling in the background as the boy brought the paper to his mother. "bring it here! okay... it was in the middle.. okay here it is, page 9. Sears... hey kiddies, call me direct on my merry Christmas telephone... M E 2-6681."

the Colonel's face went white. he looked at his watch. "is that the evening edition?"

more rustling. "...yes, sir."

"good heavens," the Colonel said to himself. Boyd strolled over to some binders on the shelves lining the back corner of the cab.

"sir, i'm so sorry, please don't hold this against us. my husband will be so upset--"

"ma'am, you haven't done anything wrong. thank you for the information."

"oh my word, i'm so sorry. i really hope my husband won't be blamed for this--"

"ma'am i'm not even going to ask for your name. we'll find a way to take care of it. thank you for the information. go enjoy your family, and have a merry Christmas."

"yes, sir. merry Christmas, sir."

she hung up. the Colonel switched off the speaker and looked at the other men, incredulous, speechless. Boyd walked to the phone on his desk with a binder in hand.

the Colonel turned to him. "who are you calling?"

"Sears."

Pepper re-entered the cab as quickly and quietly as he'd exited it, newspaper in hand. he handed it to Roberts, opened to the Sears ad. Roberts looked, then showed it to the Colonel. the Colonel looked at it, then back at Roberts. Roberts waved a hand, clueless.

"no answer." Boyd hung up the phone and slapped his phonebook binder closed.

the Colonel slid the paper down the command bench. "try that one."

Boyd dialed the number.

the red phone rang again, the alarm bell outside the cab clanging sharply. the Colonel silenced all the ringing with a quick flip of the telephone speaker switch, but said nothing.

"hello?" Boyd's voice feedbacked over the speaker. he pushed the cradle down and the call went dead.

"wellll shit." the Colonel massaged his temple. Walter picked up the paper and looked at the ad. "Roberts, get Bonner up here."

Roberts was at the door in a flash. "Bonner. front and center." Mo dashed up the stairs two and three at a time and was in the cab. he saluted the Colonel, who whipped one back.

"you know the phone lines in this place?"

"uh, yes, sir. well, a little. i haven't done anything--"

the Colonel interrupted his protest. "i know it's not you this time. calm down." the hotline phone rang again. "dammit. Boyd?"

"yes sir?"

"you're Santa. Bonner, take me and Roberts to the switchboard."

"yes sir!" and they were off. Captain Milton tapped Froggy and Airman Burke, and they followed them out of the cab and down the stairs. the rest of the brass stepped out on to the tiers, immediately consulting with one another. Pepper stood back in a corner while Walter paced. Boyd lifted the receiver, ceasing the loud hotline ringer. he closed his eyes and took a quick breath in the silence.

"hello? well hello there, my friend!" Boyd's voice, comically deep, boomed off the angled plexiglas windows overlooking the Command Center. "have you been a good boy this year? oh that's nice!"

David's heart was pounding. they'd all feared the imminent firepower of a closely matched adversary, and now his superior was doing cartoon voices to children on the phone. Walter looked at the paper, shaking his head. he passed the paper to David, and there it was — the most important secret telephone number in the whole world published in the evening paper.

"okay, i'll see what i can do. get some sleep, young man. all right, merry Christmas." he started to hang up, then remembered, "oh.. ho ho ho!" Boyd looked at David as he laid down the receiver. "this is bonkers."

immediately the phone rang again, the red bell clattering loudly off every hard surface. Boyd hesitated just long enough to stifle a laugh, then answered. "helllooo! ho ho ho." he covered the mouthpiece and whispered to Pepper. "Donaldson, can you clip the alarm bell on this thing? i don't care to listen to that all night."

"roger, sir." Pepper hustled off as Boyd immediately jumped back into character and took the young child's request.

§

carol of the bells

David left the cab in a stupor. was this a bad, weird dream? he felt the texture of the newsprint in his hand to make sure. he turned back to look though the slanted glass at Boyd on the phone.

on the top tier of the theater, Majors McKellar and Tilday plotted.

"why is the Colonel even still here?" McKellar huffed.

"he was on his way home when the bell went off."

"so we're going to leave Boyd on the phone all night? we can't put one of the airmen on it?"

"i dunno. it's technically still a classified line. if a call does come in from one of the early warning stations, it will still be on that line."

"i think the only thing coming through tonight will be several hundred phone calls from area children."

and Major Tilday chuckled. "poor Boyd."

the bell went off again as Pepper returned to the cab with his toolbox. David wanted to return to the conference room for some of that strawberry cake, but no one else was going anywhere. he wasn't going to be the first.

the Colonel and Major Roberts came back up the steps to the two other Majors. Captain Milton, behind them, headed straight into the cab. the Colonel looked annoyed. "Bonner is going reroute all incoming calls to, basically, every phone in the building. let's get airmen at every station on the tiers to answer phones. brass, too, i guess. whatever it takes." Lt. Col. Boyd quietly stepped out of the cab, a raincoat in hand. David looked to the red phone to see Captain Milton taking calls.

"that's a lot of Santas," said Major McKellar.

"maybe we're elves, then," Major Tilday offered with a chuckle. "Santa's helpers?"

"won't news get out that the phone number is the CONAD red phone?" Roberts asked, ever the pragmatist.

the Colonel thought about that for a second, then bust out laughing. it was the first smile David had seen from him today. maybe ever. "good heavens, what a PR nightmare. Barney's going to have his work cut out for him in the morning." another thought brightened his eyes. "i already know what he'll tell us: embrace it. everyone loves Santa. CONAD should definitely be on Santa's side, that will win us good favor in the eyes of the American public. Santa's helpers. that's good, Jack. we're Santa's helpers... *at CONAD*. we take their Christmas lists, and we give them Santa's current heading in return. can you have an airman draw that up?"

Boyd turned to David. David now realized Boyd was well aware he was eavesdropping, something David hadn't even been aware of. "Michaels. Santa's heading? track it for us on the pit mapboards?"

"yessir."

Boyd waited as David stood there, then shoo'd him away with a hand motion. David picked up his binder and started down the stairs, slowly realizing he had no idea how to a track an imaginary heading. he wasn't even sure what questions to ask.

at the bottom of the stairs, he laid the paper down on the first tier floor and waited on the descending parade of brass, hoping to get some more direction from Lt. Col. Boyd.

"we still need a secure line in and out, sir."

"i'm aware, Roberts. have Bonner take a lesser-used line for the time being."

"should we call the phone company and get a new line installed?" asked Major McKellar.

the Colonel looked at his watch. "at... 6:45 on Christmas Eve? yeah go ahead." Boyd handed the coat on his arm to the Colonel.

"anyone working on the holidays for the phone company is still tied up with the Pike's Peak thing anyway," Boyd reminded.

the Colonel stopped to put on his coat, and the Majors stopped with him. "this reveals yet another weakness of our current setup. just tack it on to the Crackerjack report. a temp line will be sufficient for a couple of days until we can get something better between here and SAC." everyone looked at each other. in the cab, the phone rang again, this time only a muffled flutter through the glass; no bell. "well. Boyd, the Command Center is yours. i'm headed home for some spiced wine and figgy pudding." he headed toward the tunnel. "i think i might call the radio station... tell them we spotted an unidentified flying object, guy in a red suit holding the reins." he laughed to himself. "ol' Barney's going to get a kick out of this." and he disappeared into the dark tunnel.

"Alspach!" Boyd yelled.

Howard answered. "yes sir!"

"take Gordy and Cesana and get every phone in the building up here on the tiers. Mo, do what you can to reroute all the calls going to the red phone out to all of these phones here."

"already on it, sir. i just have to take the reception switchboard from the lobby--"

"don't need the details, Bonner, just get it done. take Marston and Sollee if you need help."

"yes, sir." and Mo sauntered off, Marston and Sollee right on his heels.

"Pepper, can you dismantle this red light?"

"actually..."

all the officers on the tiers turned to look at David, who just realized he'd interrupted and contradicted his Lieutenant Colonel. Boyd raised an eyebrow at him. this wasn't a private conversation over a holiday meal. the Commanding Officer was giving orders.

"...sorry, sir. i just... thought it was kind of festive."

Boyd gave no reaction and turned back toward Pepper.

"just stop it from spinning, will you? it's giving me a headache. and get that five-and-dime silver tree from the den and bring it out here." he turned to David and raised an eyebrow again.

David smiled. "thank you, sir."

Boyd pushed past him as everyone bustled about with their job. David stood there, wondering what he should do. he figured it'd be fun to help Howard.

"Michaels."

David turned to see Roberts next to him. "yessir?"

"Santa's heading?"

"oh, right." he took his binder and headed back toward the den, where he kept his charts. he paused at the door as Howard, Gordy, and Leonard stepped out, their arms full of black, military-issue telephones. he was about to step through when a gold star nearly gored him in the eye. the star was followed by the silver fronds of a three-dollar miniature aluminum Christmas tree.

"coming through," Pepper announced, polite and quiet as always. he stepped through the doorway, dragging the cord for the spinning light behind him.

David headed for his cubicle and was startled when something moved. it was Airman Burke, pulling one ear back from a set of headphones.. "hey."

David caught his breath. "sorry, i didn't know anyone else was in here."

"Freeman stuck me down here. somebody's gotta watch the radios, apparently." Burke lifted the contents of his binder, a catalog of radio frequencies for long-distance bases across the continent, and fanned the corner as the pages fell.

"yeah. we can't all have fun."

there was a little rumble of commotion from all the ado up top, but otherwise, the den was silent.

"anything on the radio?"

"nope."

"well. okay then."

Burke dialed the radio to the next frequency on his list. "yep."

David grabbed the couple of charts he needed and headed back out.

David unrolled his charts on the table behind the big plexiglas mapboards, weighting down the corners. he grabbed a red grease pencil and unraveled the tip. Santa would come from the North Pole, right? or maybe he'd come from the east? after all, the homes in New York and Chicago would hit midnight before Colorado Springs. but who says Santa comes right at midnight? as kids, he and his sisters could never get to sleep before 1am on Christmas

Eve, and then they were usually up by 5, well before their parents were ready to get up. and once the big guy made it into the Mountain time zone, would he go north to south? or maybe a big zig-zag pattern? maybe he was putting too much thought into it. he laughed to himself at the absurdity of it all and wrote DEST CoSp (for destination Colorado Springs) over the starred home positions on the map. David had become an expert at writing backwards in the last few months, so the brass on the tiers could read the flight paths properly from the front without someone blocking the maps. it was confusing for him at first, but now he was adept at it. in fact, he'd sometimes find himself absent-mindedly signing for packages at the APO with a backwards signature.

within twenty minutes, Mo had every phone set up on the tiers, all routed from the red phone's incoming number, and they were all ringing. it took every line in the building, but the whole Command Center was abuzz with chipper chatter. Majors talked about Betsy Wetsy dolls, and Captains ho-ho-ho'd into their handsets. as soon as someone would end a call, his telephone would ring again, and back at it they would go. Mo put on some Christmas music finally, and let it play in the background. for all the commotion, this was shaping up to be an interesting night.

David smiled at them, peering through the plexiglas map. everyone seemed to be having fun. Boyd had every able body on a telephone, every body except David. his smile faded when he realized he was only watching people have fun. he went back to his charts, but it was difficult to concentrate on his work when his feelings were hurt.

soon, he had a rough flight plan hashed out, so he decided to use that as an excuse to walk the tiers and get a little closer to the action. he sketched out the pertinents on a piece of paper, grabbed a few rolls of charts to look official, and walked around the mapboard and onto the pit floor.

as he climbed the stairs, David heard all kinds of words and noises he never expected to hear in the Continental Air Defense Command Center. he found an empty chair on the first tier and sat down. he set his charts on the desk and pretended to work some calculations on his sketch while he listened to the phonecalls around him.

above him, Howard gave his jolliest old elf impression. he already had the deep voice and the good nature. David smiled, and Howard smiled right back at him, not the least bit embarrassed.

next to David were Gordy and Leonard. Leonard was mid-call as Gordy waited for his phone to ring again.

"you want your daddy to come home? and where is your daddy? Ray Barracks in Friedberg, Germany. ah, i have a friend stationed there."

Gordy threw a peanut at him. "no, you don't, you're an elf, remember?"

Leonard covered the mouthpiece. "elves can be in the military, they only work one night a year."

"that's Santa, idiot. the elves are making toys year-round--"

"guys?" they both looked at Captain Milton, manning the phone on the tier above them. "stay on task, please?"

"sorry, sir."

Howard laughed, and winked at David. David wondered what he might say to one of the children, given the chance.

Leonard pushed David's charts out of his way. "can you get this junk outta my space, Michaels?" he whispered, receiver against his shoulder.

"it's not taking up that much room."

"go do your work in your cubicle where you're supposed to." Gordy said at full volume, then answered his ringing phone.

David gathered his charts, organizing them. stalling. he didn't want to be banished to the dens tonight. just him and Burke down there together. bored out of their minds.

"Airman Michaels."

"sir?" David looked up, surprised to see Major Roberts over his shoulder.

"you have business on the tiers?"

David shot up. "sorry, sir. yes, sir. i came up to drop off a schedule of Santa's position to all the phone operators." he laid a paper with his hastily scratched notes on the corner of the desk.

Roberts raised an eyebrow.

"... and now i'm done, so..." David slowly turned and headed down the steps. Howard handed his phone to Airman Marston and fell in line behind David.

"hey," Howard called after him.

"what." David didn't even turn around.

"what's with the sourpuss."

"why are you off the phones?"

"gotta hit the head. now answer my question."

David hit the pit floor and turned to look up at the tiers. "i work hard."

"we all work hard, Michaels."

"i know, i didn't-- nevermind."

Howard yelled up the stairs. "Dickie!" Airman Marston sat up, surprised, the receiver still to his ear. "Michaels gets the next call." Marston smiled and gave a thumbs up. Howard turned to David. "you can take over my phone until i get back from the can."

"thanks," David sighed.

Howard reached across David to the first tier floor and grabbed the folded up newspaper. he winked at David and headed for the tunnel.

David smiled and hustled up the stairs just as Marston was finishing his call. Marston put down the handset into the cradle, and the phone started ringing again immediately. Marston hopped up. David sat down, took a deep breath, and picked up the phone.

"hello! merry Christmas! i'm David. i'm one of Santa's helpers. what's your name?"

"Frankie." it was the high-pitched little voice of a young boy, probably about eight years old.

"hi, Frankie. what do you want for Christmas?"

"i want a kerchief for my Cub Scout uniform."

"Cub Scouts, huh? what rank are you?"

"i'm a wolf!"

"oh that's great, Frankie."

"promise me i can have a kerchief, Santa!"

"well we'll see, have you been a good boy?"

"yes i have. but mommy says we can't get a kerchief until daddy goes back to work. so you have to bring it, Santa."

"i'm not Santa--"

"what?"

"--i'm just a helper, but i'll pass it along to the, uh, the man upstairs--"

"no, tell Santa! i want to talk to Santa!"

"i... uh... he can't.. talk now.."

Howard yanked the handset away from him. "ho ho ho! hello! have you been a good boy? you have? wonderful! well, you need to go on to sleep if you want me to stop by tonight! okay, good night, and merrrry Christmas!" Howard hung up and his performer's smile immediately disintegrated. "the hell you doin, Michaels?"

"what do you mean?"

"you don't have to actually fill the order. you just nod and say merry Christmas. hang up, take the next call. it's not that hard."

"the kid was asking for something his mom told him they couldn't afford. i'm not going to lie to him--"

"the whole thing is a lie, Michaels! there is no Santa Claus!"

a barrage of angry shushing came from the nearby phones.

Howard's line started ringing again. "didn't you do Santa in your family?"

"not really."

Howard rolled his eyes. "that explains a lot."

"sorry, but we didn't think lying to each other about an imaginary sky elf was in the true spirit of Christmas."

"i thought that was the whole basis of your religion." David spun around, angry, to see Mo standing there, going through his binder.

"i'm talking about Santa Claus."

"it's all Santa Claus, Michaels." Mo pulled out the Bible, passed David and sat in an empty chair. he threw the Bible onto the desk and lit a cigarette. David reached for the Bible, and Mo pushed it away. "nah nah nah, this is mine now. you can have it back when our shift is over."

David glared at him, then at Howard, who was already on the phone. "i thought you were going to the bathroom."

Howard covered the handset. "i did."

"that fast?'

Howard ignored him. "hello little girl! have you been a good child this year?"

"did you eat some of Gordy's hamball?"

then someone behind him cleared his throat. David turned with a sneer. "what?"

it was Major Roberts. again.

David sobered and straightened.

"i'm... sorry, sir--"

"you don't need to keep bringing paper up here. just mark it on the board. that's why we have them."

Roberts walked away, his order stated clearly. Howard leaned in.

"look, you wanted something to do tonight, right? maybe it'd be better for now to just follow the Major's orders."

David could smell the vapor of whiskey punch on his breath, like a toxic aftershave. "fine."

Howard returned to his phone call. David took his charts and slowly puttered down the metal staircase, feeling his full weight with every step. he crossed the pit floor, peering into the sharp shine on his black shoes as he strode.

back behind the map, David pulled out his grease pencils and started marking his figures onto the map. he paused, peering through the etched markings at the stadium of fellow uniforms. each of them were laughing, snacking, and enjoying each other's company, fueled in part by the punch, David guessed.

he could also see into the den. lit dimly by a lone desklamp, Airman Burke scratched the back of his head.

David peeled a layer from his grease pen and began writing.

§

coming to town

David made a few markings, then flipped through his binder. it was full of notes from Operation Crackerjack, a log of everything they'd been through that day. the first warning call had come in the afternoon, and it was forty-five minutes before most of the watchposts were filled along the northern border with their civilian volunteers, the Civil Air Patrol. the expectation was for bombers to attack from the coasts, and so preparations to date had left lots of gaps up north, lots of room for Soviet bombers to get through. the USSR would soon develop planes that could fly farther, would soon have aircraft carriers. if the U.S. was building ice stations, the Soviets were no doubt doing the same, bringing the front lines closer and closer. David looked at the map on the glass in front of him and made calculations, jotting notes in the margins, careful to keep them separate from notes made by the Lieutenant Colonel.

David began reconstructing the timeline of the drill in his mind. with a blue ink pen, he scratched out a map on a sheet of paper, a near-perfect outline of the US with blue dots for CONAD, SAC, DC, New York, LA, and Bowling Green, where his family was. in black, he marked watchtowers along the coasts and the

Canadian border, consulting the huge see-through map in front of him. in red, he drew in planes, each representing squadrons of aircraft, detailed doodles of Tupelov bombers and MiG fighters. he drew red arcs to mark the far ranges of the aircraft, information he had burned into his memory from basic. he'd traced so many arcs on paper and glass, he didn't even need a compass any more. everywhere there was a space between the black watchtowers, he colored red — places where hundreds of Soviet aircraft could penetrate US airspace, that blue ceiling over farms, banks, burger joints, and grade schools. he set down his red pencil and looked at his map.

"good grief, there's holes everywhere."

"the thing about glass, is you can see that map from the front, too." it startled David, and he turned to see Lt. Col. Boyd strolling out of shadows. he caught his breath and pointed at the back of the map with his wax pen.

"yes sir. just don't wanna get my easts and wests mixed up. easier this way."

Boyd nodded, unconvinced. he handed David a cup of water.

"thank you, sir."

"if you want a shift working the phones, i'll swap you out with one of the others."

"oh, no sir. thank you, sir," David said, taking a sip of cool water. "i have a lot to do here."

Boyd looked at David's drawing. "did you do this by hand?"

"yes, sir."

"what am i looking at?"

"well, i was building this table, sir, like you asked before dinner. arrival times at the civil posts. and. well. forty-five minutes is a long time. and, even once the posts were manned, we just... well, we've got some gaps still."

"we're aware. we're filling them as fast as we can. same goes for our friends in Canada. but, it's a lot of space to cover."

"yes, sir." David looked at all the red on his page. "we don't stand much of a chance, do we, sir?"

Boyd took a deep breath. "we're doing everything we can." Boyd sat down next to him. "the Soviets lie about everything, but even with conservative estimates, the number of planes they have..." Boyd stared at David's map.

"...sir?"

Boyd blinked and looked back at David. "just... we're doing everything we can."

"sir, i'm not an analyst, but... i don't think we did so well during this drill."

"well, that's what drills are for. to find points of failure. better to find them in a drill than in the real thing."

"yes, sir. that's true, i guess. well. i hope we get these warning systems closed up before the Soviets build a plane that can fly 10,000 miles."

"the Soviets have the V2."

"German rocket."

"that's right."

"it's only got a range of 1500 miles, they'd basically have to be in Vancouver--"

"they're not building better planes. they're building bigger rockets."

David's blood went cold at the thought. what good would a civilian with binoculars be against a giant V2 headed for Pike's Peak.

"sir, i heard the Russians have a true thermonuclear bomb. " Boyd offered no response, no reaction. "that they had a successful test last month. maybe close to two megatons."

Boyd stared hard at David. "airman, i can neither confirm nor deny."

David looked at his map. "how are we going to win that kinda war, sir?"

"we're not fighting that war yet, Airman Michaels." Boyd breathed. "not yet."

a loud laugh broke the tension. David looked up into the tiers where his buddies were working, but having a good time. Howard was entertaining a couple of the guys with a story while they waited on calls. the rest of Santa's helpers plugged their open ear, straining to hear the children amid the commotion. Howard slid down the stair handrail, and Gordy chortled, answering his phone as Howard disappeared into the tunnel. the calls were coming non-stop, and picking up steam. every phone was on a call or ringing. and the guys in the tiers were having the night of their life. David ran his thumb over the ridges on his slide ruler as he watched them.

"why don't you head up there, Michaels."

"oh, no, sir," David repeated, without the excuses.

"they're pretty tough on you sometimes." Boyd was getting at something, but David wasn't sure what.

"all my life," David said, "i was taught to live a certain way. i was taught, live this way and it will make the Lord happy and people will respect you."

"not everyone was taught that."

Howard re-appeared in the tunnel entrance, paper cup in hand, full of punch once again.

"yes, sir, i know that. and. i don't much care what they think, i guess. but. it makes me wonder if the part about making the Lord happy was true either."

Boyd considered David's confession.

"do you know why i'm here?"

"because you called the Colonel a hothead during last week's briefing?"

"at CONAD," Boyd clarified, annoyed. "as a lieutenant colonel."

"oh. uh, no sir?"

"i was chosen. i was selected to be here. i studied and worked hard, i put in the time, the hours, i made sacrifices. it was noticed by people that matter. and i was promoted over and over and now, i'm here. and what we do here is important."

"yes, sir."

Boyd stared at him, waiting for a response.

"i'm.. proud of you, sir?"

Boyd shook his head. "you're here, too, Michaels."

"i'm just a boardsman, sir."

Boyd grabbed David's map and held it up to him. "we've got boardsmen in every Air Force Base in the country. most of them would be as skilled at being a dishwasher in the galley. you were sent here because someone thought you were up to the challenge of what we do here. you were picked because you have something we need."

"did you pick me, sir?"

"no."

"oh."

"but i would have if i'd been given the chance." Boyd looked at David's map. "especially if i'd seen this." Boyd looked it over. "we should include this in the report."

"i'll make a clean one."

"a clean one? this one looks like it was done by an architect."

"i'll make a clean one, sir." David took the map from him and tucked it into his binder.

"David, i think there's one important thing holding you back."

"yes, sir?"

"you're not a team player."

"i'm sorry, sir, i don't mean to be--"

"will you just shut up for a second? i don't mean you don't want to be a team player, or that you're a loner. but the fact of the matter is, we have to work as a single unit here. and right now, the rest of your unit is enjoying some jingles and a little Christmas joy. you don't have to join them, but i do want you to work with them." Boyd reached for a sheet of David's paper and his blue ink pen and began writing. he jotted a quick scribble and handed it back to David. "this is your new assignment for the evening. and you don't have to compromise your values, or even leave your current post. and then when you're done, you can get back to these logs."

David looked at the paper. "are you serious, sir?"

Boyd tossed the grease pencils to him. "it's an order."

the mapboards his canvas, David sketched an outline in black, imagining the layering of colors as it would look on the other side of the glass. he added white highlights, then began adding color all around.

Howard noticed first. he moseyed down the metal stairs and stood in front of the big glass map, watching his buddy on the other side.

David looked at him, and kept drawing.

as Howard sipped his punch, others took notice and began pointing. a few more came down the stairs to see it up close. David had a immense level of detail in his drawing, ever feature told some story, hinted at some motion, evoked some feeling. he'd learned it from studying the Norman Rockwell covers on the Saturday Evening Post magazines back home.

the phones were still going at full tilt. even so, Mo turned up the music from the record player, some 45s from a big band Air Force collection that had just come out a few months earlier. and soon, every elf in the tiers was standing and dancing like it was a Christmas sock hop. Mo propped the speaker up, aimed at the tiers, and Glenn Miller had everyone gyrating while they answered calls and watched David work.

David put some finishing touches and stepped back to look. he could see through his imagination what they were seeing on the other side of the glass; his side looked like the back of a cross-stitch, a messy impression of the work on top, betraying the craft behind the art. it was like a magic trick and only David could see how it was done. with bold red, black lines, lots of color accents, David admired his drawing of Santa in his reindeer-pulled sleigh, toys spilling from his sack, glimmering stars trailing behind it all showing his journey from the north pole.

"whoa!"

"that's spiffy, chief."

Boyd smiled at him through the glass, then headed back to the cab. there was some smattered applause as everyone talked to their neighbor, pointing out details and admiring David's handiwork. David had a thought and held up a finger, and the room quieted down, save the music. with two white grease pencils, he wrote in cursive — backwards — in one long stroke, "Merry Christmas", and accented it with two exclamation points. he smiled as he stepped back. everyone cheered. David beamed.

Howard stepped to the glass and pushed his paper cup against it.

David reached down for his water and tapped it to Howard's, the thick plexiglas between them. "cheers."

Howard winked, his cheeks pink from punch and whiskey.

over his shoulder, Mo smirked at David. "not bad, Michaels," he said, and gave him a thumbs up.

David raised his cup as a toast to Mo. maybe he'd try some punch after all. in any case, being a stick in the mud all night hadn't won him any friends.

Mo headed back to his crate of records and pulled an album. soon they were all dancing to "Santa Baby" while they continued the phone calls. Marston and Sollee brought some of the food from the fishbowl up into the tiers. the tiers were usually reserved for officers and important men. but most of them were off-duty tonight, home with their families, soon to be fast asleep without a care in the world. so for tonight, even the youngest airmen would kick their feet up on some Major's station and gnaw on a turkey leg. Mo enjoyed his party from the shadow of the tier wall, leaning against the doorframe of the utility room as he peeled an orange into a small wastebasket, his tools and David's Bible at his feet.

David gathered up his charts, ruler, and pens to take them back into the den. it seemed clear no one was really interested in getting any real work done tonight. the whole phone thing had thrown everyone for a loop.

in the den, Burke sat at his cubicle, still dialing through radio frequencies.

"anything happening?"

"nope," Burke replied, turning a page in his binder.

a commotion came through the tunnel. it was Howard and Marston, laughing. Howard poked his head through the door of the den. "what are you two doing?"

"working," Burke said with a bristle.

"he's listening for radio communications. where are y'all going?"

"break room. gonna bring the punch out."

"i'll give you a hand," David said, asserting himself at the opportunity. he quickly dumped his supplies on the nearest desk.

Howard looked at him, surprised. "uh, no. don't do that. actually... Burke!"

"yeah."

"come give us a hand! Marston, relieve Burke. he needs to have some fun."

"what about me?" David protested.

"you keep making your own fun."

Marston squeezed into Burke's cubicle. "i'm relieving you? what are you doing?"

"monitoring the radio."

"how are you listening to the radios with no headset?"

"i was tired of wearing the headset, and no one else was in here, so i switched it over to the PA."

"the speaker?" Howard said, suddenly terrified.

"yeah, the--" Burke turned and pointed to the unpainted square on the wall behind him where the speaker had been, two freshly-clipped wires hanging limply beneath it. "oh shit." he quickly grabbed his headset and threw it on his head. he started clicking through the frequencies, listening for a few seconds to each one.

"what was he thinking," Howard said, in disbelief.

"it's fine," David said. "no one's doing any work anyway. the phones are all over the place."

"which is why we need the radio. as a backup for the phones. that's why Freeman sent him down here." oh. that made sense. suddenly David understood why Howard was scared, and that made him scared, too. how was it that Howard always could see all the way to the end of the thought process? *why can't i do that,* David thought.

Burke finally stopped on one and his eyes grew huge. he yanked down the microphone from where it sat atop the radio unit. "this is CONAD Command Center radio control. we read you. come in." he listened, his face tightening with each second that passed. David, Howard, and Marston hovered, frozen.

Burke pressed the headphones into his head. "dammit!" he shouted, pulling back one ear. "Barter Island has been trying to get through for the past hour."

Howard immediately bolted for the pit floor.

"what's the problem?" David asked Burke, ice rocketing through his arteries.

"they can only give details over a secure line. they've been getting a busy signal here for the past hour."

Marston and David sprinted out of the den, rounded the pit floor, and looked up the stairs. Howard was already up top, banging on the door of the cab. Major Roberts yanked it open.

"what the hell, Alspach."

"Barter Island has been trying to get through to us for an hour."

Roberts' face went white. he quickly yelled to the pit floor. "Bonner! do these phones call out?"

"sir? why are you trying to call out?"

"do they or don't they, Tech Sergeant?"

Mo sputtered. "i.. you can give it a try, if you find one that's not ringing." they were all ringing.

"get us a line in the cab. now." and Roberts slammed the door in Howard's face. Mo rushed past David and Marston and hustled into the guts of cables and pipes under the tiers.

David panted.

Marston looked scared. "what's happening?? where's Barter Island?"

"Alaska."

§

deck the halls

the clanging alarm bell startled everyone with a few bursts. David could see Roberts touching the wires together that Pepper had clipped a few moments ago. the noise seized everybody's attention. Roberts gave a wave through the glass, and brass in the tiers hurried upstairs.

Mo emerged from the utility room. "Major! tell Colonel Boyd his desk phone should be a free line!" he shouted. McKellar nodded as he slipped into the cab and shut the door behind him. Mo turned off his turntable, then stepped back into the guts, pulling cables and trimming wire.

through the cab glass, David could see everyone talking to Boyd, breaking off and talking to each other, scrambling for binders on the shelves; it was a whirl of bodies in there, just short of panic. Boyd was on the phone, looking serious. he handed it off to McKellar and crossed the cab.

Boyd appeared at the door and jousted a finger toward the phones. "one man for every two phones. keep calm, keep taking calls. Pepper, take over the radios in the den. Burke's caused enough problems for the night. the rest of you, to the pit," and he disappeared back into the cab. Pepper hustled down into the den to relieve Burke. Froggy, Leonard, and Gordy took two or three phones each, sending the younger airmen to the floor.

"do we go to our cubicles?" David asked Howard.

"to do what?" he replied.

David didn't have an answer.

"just hold tight. we're about to get orders. hopefully it's nothing."

Major Roberts exited the cab onto the top of the stairwell, shutting the cab door behind him. he pushed past Howard and slid down the stair rails, passing the airmen on his way down. he landed in a run and jogged to David.

"Michaels. we need maps."

"sir, what's going on?"

"Arctic Circle. Alaska."

"what's happening?"

"and Canada."

".. what province?"

"all of them."

"sir..."

"go, Michaels."

"Canada?"

David turned and headed back into the dens, weaving his way through the cubicles. at the radio, Pepper scoured every frequency for any more missed distress calls. David pulled out big flat drawers from the cabinets behind his desk. topographical maps? aeronautical charts? population surveys? he just started pulling whatever he had. whatever was happening was serious business, and he obviously wasn't going to be on the in. Fairbanks. Clear Station. Vancouver airport. as he turned to set Saskatchewan on his desk, he was surprised to see Airman Marston and Airman Sollee.

"Howard told us to help you bring everything to the floor." he loaded up their arms, grabbed what he could, and followed them back into the theater.

there were no tables, just a few hundred square feet of floor space. they dumped everything in a pile on one end and started constructing a crude world map out of what they had. some were this scale, some were that, and David still didn't know why they needed any of them. Howard was on the floor. he knelt to help David unroll British Columbia.

"there's a plane."

"what? how do you--"

"Roberts told me. the Alaska base thought they saw something, but weren't sure. when they couldn't get through to us--"

"oh no.." Burke looked as if he was going to be sick. Howard ignored him.

"--they panicked, and sent two F-86s to check it out. couldn't find anything."

"so what," David said. "probably just MiGs on a surveillance run."

"you got peanut butter in your ears, Michaels? it's in Canada. how's a MiG gonna get all the way into Canada?"

Boyd appeared at the cab's entrance. "where's Bonner?"

"Mo!" Howard yelled.

Mo appeared, sweaty, from the guts under the tiers. "what?"

Howard pointed to the cab.

Mo saw Boyd and immediately straightened. "yessir?"

"get an outside line to... shit. Michaels, i need a trajectory. sighting was..." he turned to the cab. Walter was in the doorway, binder in hand.

"around 18 hundred 30, sir"

"1830, Canadian border. we have to guess at where it crossed and where it came from." Boyd looked over the airmen standing in the pit. "airmen, Airman First Class Michaels is your superior for the next few hours. do whatever he tells you."

"where's it headed, sir?" David asked, but Boyd was gone, the cab door clunking shut behind him.

"guess you'll have to guess that, too." Howard sighed.

"that's a lot of guessing," David whispered.

"i'll get a line ready so we can call whoever we need... which is what i was doing anyway..." Mo muttered, slipping back into the guts of cables and piping next to the den.

David turned to see the young airmen — only a few months his junior — looking at him, silent, waiting on his instruction.

David stared back, then looked at Howard, behind them. Howard should be in charge. Howard was considered "next in line". Howard stood tall and straight as an oak, arms crossed, and lifted an eyebrow. Howard was waiting, too.

his lips and mouth drying in the silence. whatever the other group was coming up with, it all depended on David's timeline, and an accurate timeline would only come from the instructions he gave out to these young men in front of him. these new subordinates were counting on him. his peers were counting on him. Boyd was counting on him. SAC, the Pentagon, the White House, America, the whole world.

the children.

Frankie.

David imagined the faceless little voice laughing with joy tomorrow morning, looking for his new kerchief.

suddenly David was 14 again, in the woods. the pitch black cold rang his body like the thump of a cast iron kettle. his wet breath escaping in a cloud in front of him, illuminated from underneath by campfire. young boys added wood, and the heat swelled from within and without as they worked and the fire grew. David, Hoot Owl Patrol Leader, gave instructions and managed the small project. as the bonfire roared, the front of their uniforms turned thin and crisp, warming the damp skin underneath. as the nighttime chill swirled across the backs of their knees, sweat beaded on their foreheads. they raised three fingers into the air to recite. "on my honor, i will do my best..."

"David?" Airman Marston looked at him with concern.

David was fully grown again, standing in his uniform under the air conditioning and dim fluorescent lights. David could not save the world. but he could mange this task. he took a deep breath and stared at all of his maps in disarray on the floor. "what kind of plane?" David shouted toward the cab.

he turned for an answer, but Boyd was already gone.

Walter stepped off the last stair, his binder tucked up under his arm. he looked like he'd aged ten years in the last five minutes. "it was high. that's probably why we haven't heard from any airports. well. that and the phone thing. assume 40,000."

"bomber," said Howard. and all the airmen on the floor froze, stunned at the implication. David thought about the thick rug on his living room carpet back home, how it itched him as he lay on it, listening to the radio with his mom and dad, his grandmother's clock tocking loudly in the background.

"guys..." Walter snapped them all back into the present.

Burke spoke up, eager to redeem his mistake. "Tupolevs have a high service ceiling. probably a Tu-4, or the new one."

"the 16," Howard said.

"i'll go get the book on it," and Marston's spry blue uniform jetted into the den.

"wait a minute, do we know for sure this is Russian?" asked Airman Sollee.

Howard threw him a skeptical frown. "what are you talking about?"

"they don't even know what they saw. it could have been... a meteor. maybe it was a passenger jet--"

"a passenger jet?" Howard asked, caustic. "at 40,000 feet?"

Sollee shrugged and pointed at Walter. "he just said *assume* 40,000 feet."

"you really think it's a passenger jet?" David asked.

Sollee sighed. "i don't *think* it is, but i hope it is."

"all they said was, they saw a plane," Burke said, stepping in to defend Sollee.

"no." Walter pushed himself into the middle of the quarreling group. "they said they're pretty sure it was a plane. and they didn't 'see' it. it showed up on radar. they're installing radars on the DEW line."

"if it's on radar, then how'd they lose it?" David asked, incredulous, and everyone tensed.

"this was a construction crew. the radar isn't even operational yet. it blipped as they were testing something. it's not even hooked into anything else yet. it was a blip, they reported it to Barter Island, Barter Island called Anchorage. they discussed it, they tried calling us. by the time they moved on it, it was long gone."

"they didn't get a visual?" asked Sollee.

"it was far away. and, it's night."

"i thought this happened hours ago. when's sunset?"

"up there? November."

Howard laughed to himself.

"this is funny?" David was genuinely un-jolly.

"a little," Howard said, irritated. "we don't even know what to argue about."

"he's got a point, guys." everyone's posture relaxed when Walter spoke. "it could be a lost passenger jet, it could be something private, it could be a weather event, or a technical glitch. or it could be something Soviet. Boyd and Mo are working on making contact. if it's a lost passenger jet, we'll get it handed off soon enough, and everyone can get back into their punch and Perry Como. if it was a meteor, it's now part of the Great White North. the only thing that concerns us is if it's Soviet. so until we're ordered otherwise, we assume it is, and plan appropriately."

everyone breathed.

"so what are the Soviet options?" David looked around at his team.

"isn't that what brass is supposed to be figuring out?" Sollee asked.

"they are," Howard said. "but we have to make some assumptions to track this blip."

"MiGs from the ground?" Sollee asked.

"our radars are still garbage at low altitude," David said. "if it's MiGs, who knows how many have snuck through."

Burke nervously hoped this was his out. "MiGs are short range. nothing for us to worry about here, right?"

"maybe just doing reconnaissance, and already back home in Khurba." Sollee offered.

"hang on." David pushed maps aside with his shoe, searching. "Walter, where was this construction crew?"

"Northwest Territories."

"that's too far inland. Howard's right, i don't think a MiG would ever make it back." he made eye contact with Howard.

Howard may have been right in the first place about it being a bomber.

Marston returned with a binder, slapping through the sheathed pages. "okay... Tupolev Tu-16 bomber. service ceiling estimated 49,000 ft, top speed around 650 miles an hour. range, 4,200 miles." he held out the binder for David, who walked past him. Howard took the binder and unclasped the page in question. David scanned his charts scattered across the floor, and pointed.

"that one. there. this one. that one, i guess." as he pointed at each, Sollee and Marston grabbed them and pushed aside the rest. Walter walked back to the stairs.

"wait, hang on. Northwest Territories?" Howard said. "i thought you said it was at the Canadian border."

"northern border," Walter said. "Arctic Circle."

"north pole?"

Walter threw up his hands, unsure, then headed back up to the cab.

David rubbed his temple. "we haven't talked much about an attack from the Arctic Circle, and we certainly haven't planned for it."

"they don't have a fleet for it," Howard said, although it sounded like more of a question.

"unless they're farther ahead than we thought they were," said Sollee.

"and i don't have a map for it," David said.

"there's one in the lobby." Airman Burke seemed happy to have an idea to contribute.

"the tapestry?" Howard asked.

Burke shrugged. "it's a map."

"get it," David said.

"on it." Marston and Burke bolted for the exit.

"it's not even to scale, is it?" Howard objected.

"it's... a map. i can put the pieces together here. but i need a bird's eye view of the Arctic Circle. Sollee, hang these in order there next to the glass. and hang the rest of them where we can use them."

"what do we hang them with."

Howard stepped forward as David scrolled through the curated set of maps. "packing tape. electrical tape. thumbtacks. chewing gum. your shoelaces. whatever. just be industrious and make it happen." Sollee bounced off after a solution. Howard sidled up to David. "you think his mom still lays his clothes out for him?"

"i need my tools. and a clipboard," David said.

Howard stood, staring at David, then stepped off toward the den shaking his head. from the tunnel, the airmen brought a wooden frame of the tapestry into the pit, the Arctic Circle over the Central US and Canada, Soviet Siberia inverted above it.

"there's two more," Marston said. he chuckled. "the guards in the lobby were flipping out when we--"

David cut him off. "prop it up front and center. we'll use the real maps as insets of this."

Marston's chuckle turned cold. as he headed back out, Mo stepped out of the guts, a spool of cable and wire clippers in his hands.

"i stole another line for calling out," Mo said, "we just need a phone for it."

"hey can you give me a hand with this table?"

"yes, sir," Mo mocked, following him behind the plexiglas.

"sorry, Tech Sergeant. the rest of my team is off doing stuff, and this is easier with two people."

"you team," he mocked again, as they pulled the table around to the pit floor. "if you're done with me, Airman, i'll get us a telephone."

"thanks," David said, pretending not to notice his attitude. Mo tossed his spool and clippers on the table and sauntered off.

Howard returned with David's pouch of grease pencils, his slide ruler, a clipboard, and a box of pushpins and set them all on the table. "you ordering your Tech Sergeant around now?"

"he was helping me move the table."

"i saw." Howard stood next to him, looking at the maps with him.

"4200 miles." it escaped David's lips, a betrayed thought.

"what about it," Howard said, handing over the tools.

"range of the Tu-16. 4200 miles. even from the northern-most islands of Siberia, 4200 miles... half of that is 2100 miles... that barely gets you into Canada."

Marston and Burke returned with the western portion of the tapestry, propping it up next to the first section.

"we'll they're... probably not going to Canada."

David turned to Howard. "that's my point. it also means they don't plan on going back."

that confirmed it. the bomber — if that's what it was — was on a suicide mission. as Sollee hung the charts, David measured distances, converting the scales, scratching figures on a notepad. as Marston and Burke brought in the final section, David stuck a couple of pushpins in his lips and grabbed Mo's spool of phone cord. he stuck one pushpin through the loose end of the cord, then pinned it into the Siberian isles, letting the spool unravel to the ground. he ripped off corners from his notepad with distances scrawled on them and taped them to the cable. northern Siberia, 0. northern Canada, 1440. US border, 3500.

he paused as he measured and scratched his last figure, 4200. Howard watched. David tore the sheet and taped it to the cable. he swung it to the left, then slowly to the right until his suspicions proved to be true. he took the other pushpin from his lips and pinned it into Colorado Springs.

§

while shepherds watched

Howard's breath evaporated, and he ran his hand back through his rough blonde hair. David looked over at Airman Sollee, who'd stopped in the middle of hanging a map, staring at the last marker. he looked at David.

"you have a job, airman. keep at it."

quaking, Sollee returned to his work. David reached for the wire clippers.

"okay now what." Howard began pacing in front of the tapestry, right behind David.

David clipped off the wire below the last marker. "i need to reverse this so we can get a countdown."

"a countdown, jeepers."

"if it crossed into mainland Canada at 1830, it's almost to the US border by now." he retrieved Mo's spool from the floor and returned it and the clippers to the table.

"how long."

"hour. give or take."

David spun on a heel and ascended to the cab. Boyd met him at the door.

"what do you have?"

"we've got maybe an hour. probably coming through Alberta and Montana. probably headed here."

"of course it's headed here," Boyd confirmed, descending the stairs. David followed, and the other officers were close behind. "Mo!"

"yes, sir. right here." Mo pushed through from behind them with an avocado green telephone in hand.

"you got us a line?" Boyd asked. Mo lifted the telephone in his hand. "great."

with his other hand, Mo grabbed a cable from the floor. one end of it extended far back into the guts, and the free end in his hand was a colorful fray of insulated copper wiring. he set the phone on the table, then began twisting wires, connecting color to color. he trimmed the excess and tossed the scraps into the small wastebasket by the utility room as he sat down beside it.

"we need numbers," Boyd urged. "who are we calling? we need a visual on this thing."

David rushed to the tapestry, scanning the charts Sollee had taped up. "start with... Calgary." David called out, checking the notes on his clipboard for calculations. "if we're lucky, it's still near there. that'd give us another half hour."

"and if we're not lucky?"

David searched another map. "Helena? Billings?"

"how long?"

David calculated in his head. "50 minutes, give or take."

"dear God, please let us be lucky," Burke said.

"someone get us the tower at Calgary, Alberta," Boyd said. Howard looked to Marston, who took the hint and was off again into the den.

"any chance Calgary is the target?" Sollee asked.

"why?" Roberts asked. "what's the play?"

Sollee had no answer. David fished for one, hoping it could be true, but other than it being a big city, it had no major strategic value.

"i can appreciate the notion," Roberts said. "but we need to accept the fact that they're headed for us."

"remember, we need visual," Boyd said. "it's probably above the airport radar. Michaels, once we get a visual, adjust your timeline. and keep adjusting it along the way. right now, we don't know airspeed, we don't know altitude, we don't even know if it's a bomber."

Majors and Captains came to the pit floor. Roberts lingered on the first tier, leaning on the railing as he looked down at the maps.

"if it is a bomber," Boyd continued, "they won't be alone. at the very least, the rest of the fleet won't be far behind. we need to reach out to every early warning post on the coasts and the U.S./Canadian border with every piece of communications we have."

Mo stood up, grimy, black grease on his sleeves and fingers, and sighed. "i've spent the whole afternoon re-routing the few telephone numbers we have to the phones on the tiers, and now you want them back?"

"national security takes precedence over Christmas lists, Bonner." Major Roberts' voice landed from the tier above. but Boyd held up a hand.

"wait. keep men on the calls for now. our whole existence is to keep the peace. right now part of that means these children sleeping peacefully."

"sir--" Roberts complained.

Boyd talked over him, "besides that line isn't secure any more. and we don't even know what we're chasing yet. let's not panic.

Mo, keep this line working and open for us. Donaldson, get a couple more lines working in the cab."

"uh, Pepper's on the short wave in the dens," Howard said.

Boyd looked around. "well-- get him out here. with the radio." Sollee hustled into the dens after Pepper. "when they get out here, Majors McKellar and Tilday, Captains Freeman and Milton, Lieutenant Demonbreun... take the cab, and use the short wave. reach out to every Alaskan and Canadian base and Civil Air Patrol tower you can, since they can't call in to us. we have to get an idea of what else is out there. do what you can with short wave radio, but be cautious over the open air. have Pepper get more phone lines up there so you can talk securely."

"yessir," McKellar chirped, as he and most of the rest of the brass headed back up into the cab. Roberts stayed, leaning against a desk on the first tier. Captain Milton leaned out of the cab to set the red phone — still ringing like the phones on the tiers — outside the door. Marston returned with the Canadian tower directory, handing it to Boyd.

"question, sir?" Howard asked with his finger in the air.

"what is it," Boyd responded, flipping through the directory.

"any chance this is phase two of Crackerjack?"

"you mean a drill?"

Howard was sharp. and David hoped he was right. Burke leaned forward. David bet he hoped Howard was right, too.

Roberts crossed his arms and rubbed his chin with his thumb. "we are technically still within the originally proposed drill window, no?"

Boyd winced a half-concession. "it would be news to me."

"you didn't know when the last drill was going to go down."

"no, but i knew that it would, and had a sense of what kind of drill. this is nothing we've talked about or planned for."

"maybe that's the point, sir," Howard said. "phase one, test our strengths. phase two, test our weaknesses."

Roberts huffed. "if 'phase one' was meant to test our strengths, we're in trouble."

"that's enough, Major," Boyd said.

while David himself had realized the drill had revealed massive shortcomings, the public face of it was 'total success'. David didn't like this kind of inherent dishonesty in the secrecy of military life, but he understood it was to protect the public at large, keeping them feeling good about Continental Air Defense. but it was also to keep the money flowing from Congress, and that felt a little less like national security, and a little more like lying.

"the point is," Boyd continued, "either way, drill or not, our response is the same. treat it just like the real thing."

"big difference," said Mo, "i don't melt at the end of a drill."

David was tired of his eternal gloom. "if we do our jobs well, we won't melt at the end of the real thing either."

"wrong," Mo shot back. "when it eventually hits the fan — and it will, and maybe this is it — we will be toast. that's guaranteed."

"it's not guaranteed," Howard said.

SLAM! everyone froze as the open directory binder slid to a stop on the table.

"the arguing isn't helpful," Boyd said, almost a whisper. David studied his face. he was one of the few people he knew who could command a squad with a quiet voice. "treat it like a drill. if we die, we die. we all knew that was a possibility."

the silence hung heavy.

Boyd spun the directory toward Walter and tapped on a number. Walter picked up the receiver.

while Walter dialed, the Lieutenant Colonel stepped closer to the tapestries. David followed him, trying to read his mind.

"if it's Soviet and headed here," Boyd posited, "it won't be the only one. Alspach, Marston, prepare a list of every coastal base and see if they've been trying to reach us."

"we need the US directory," Howard said to Marston, who jetted off into the dens.

David looked over California and New York on his tapestries. "can't SAC stop them at the coasts? we've prepared for that."

"Strategic Air Command gets intel from us, and right now, we don't have any. as soon as we hear from Calgary, i need to report everything we know to SAC, even if it's nothing." Boyd took a long look at the tapestry, then paced the floor, clicking and unclicking his pen. Howard sidled up behind David to look at the map.

"this isn't good, Howard," David whispered.

"we just had a drill on this. if we just follow protocol--"

"i've been going over data from Crackerjack. they're saying it was a success, which i guess is subjective. the truth is, if your measure of success is keeping out Soviet bombers..."

Howard leaned in.

"we're still assessing the data, but i'm guessing... thirty percent?"

"thirty percent of their fleet can get through?"

David shook his head. "we could *stop* thirty percent."

Howard's jaw dropped. "*seventy* percent of their aircraft--"

"--will reach their intended target." David finished.

Marston reappeared with another binder. behind him, Pepper and Sollee emerged from the den with one of the short wave radios and hefted it up the stairs toward the cab.

"anything new on the radios, Donaldson?"

"not a peep," Pepper said, straining.

"Calgary airport hasn't seen or heard anything," Walter announced. "RCAF is scrambling four pairs of Sabres out of Lincoln Park in four directions to try to get a visual for us."

"sir, is that a good sign or a bad sign?" Sollee asked.

"it's a no sign," Walter said. "airport radar doesn't look above 35k. it's too dark to see from the ground, and too far away to hear. we'll just have to wait until someone sees something next."

"so we wait on RCAF," Boyd said, fidgeting with his pen.

"sir, we ought to do the same from our base in Malstrom." David walked to his aeronautical chart of Montana. "but... they should look... east. over closer to Billings."

"Walter."

"yessir." and Walter volleyed to Marston, who was already looking up the number. Walter pulled a small pad from the back of his binder to make notes.

"on it, sir."

Boyd massaged his forehead. "okay, i need SAC on standby, asap. Mo?"

"line to SAC?" Mo asked. Boyd nodded. "give me about 90 seconds." Mo ran down the long phone wire back into the guts. Boyd tossed his pen onto the table.

"one plane from the north pole." Boyd said, shaking his head.

"what's the play, sir," David asked.

"we don't have a play for this," Boyd conceded. "but we oughta be able to drop whatever it is into the nearest pasture. a simple seek and destroy. if there's enough time left."

Burke sat, visibly nauseated. David, Howard, and Boyd stared at the tapestry. nearest pasture. some of this was wilderness. a lot of it was farms, like the one David grew up on. what were the chances it would land on some farmer's house while his family slept?

Mo reappeared with another long phone line and a black, no-dial telephone covered in dust. "pick it up and it rings." he pulled a handkerchief from his back pocket and wiped the dust away.

"ah, Bonner--"

"it's clean, sir."

Walter hung up the green phone. "Malstrom is sending out a squadron toward the heading we're assuming. timeline could be tight to intercept if it's closer than we think."

"i need the green phone," Boyd sighed. Walter brought it closer. "the Colonel is not going to like being woken up by this."

"one plane," David repeated. he turned to Boyd. "sir, what do you think they have?"

Boyd looked at David's artwork peeking out from under the maps taped to the plexiglass. "i doubt it's a sack full of toys."

" 'Joe-4' ?" Howard asked, referring to the latest of the Soviet test bombs named after their former dictator.

" 'Third Idea'," David said, certain the Soviets were ready to implement their newest iteration, RDS-37 — a fully thermonuclear bomb.

Boyd laid his hand on the green telephone receiver, his other hand on the black phone to SAC. "may be."

"i thought most of the new test bombs were installations," Howard said, "like about the size of a semi trailer."

Walter shook his head. "RDS-37 was air-mobile from the start, if we can trust the reports. they've only just tested it for the first time a month ago. we're still getting reports in on it, some of which claim it's a hoax."

David and Boyd looked at each other. so much for 'neither confirm nor deny'.

"even if it's real," Walter continued. "it's hard to believe they made another so quickly."

"unless they made two to begin with," Roberts said.

Boyd's fingertips were white, his weight resting on the handsets. "well. even if it's some version of an older bomb, or even standard munitions... whatever they have... they only have to destroy our building."

David looked around the stadium theater, and it suddenly felt very small. his gaze fell upon Leonard and Gordy in the tiers, still talking on the phones, still fielding requests from all the good little boys and girls of the town, visions of sugar plums waiting to greet them in their sleep.

"i mean, good grief, we've already been effectively disabled by a newspaper ad," Roberts said.

"but it's likely whatever they have will take most of the town with us," David said somberly.

Boyd nodded. "count on it," he said, and lifted the green receiver.

David watched him dial. he wanted to push him down and take the phone from him and call his mother.

"damn." Boyd hung up the phone. "busy."

" now what?" Walter asked.

Boyd rapped his fingers on the SAC line handset. "we need actionable intelligence. who's talking to someone with eyes on this plane?"

"once the Canadians find it, we could possibly get one of the Sabres on high frequency with the short wave," Mo said. "it's not secure, but we could talk to them directly."

"make it happen," Boyd said, and lifted the black receiver. Mo shot up into the cab.

David looked at Burke. he was sitting against the den wall, face pale, staring at the floor. David wondered if he looked the same. he wanted to be somewhere else. anywhere else. but especially with his family. he didn't care any more about the farm or the fire or Christmas dinner. he just wanted to be with them. he wished he could fly away at forty thousand feet for hundreds of miles, scoop up his family and just keep going until they ended up someplace safe. was there any such place? Colorado Springs had been chosen for CONAD because it was so interior, in the heart of the safest country in the world. if they weren't safe any more, was anyone anywhere?

"but that heading is only an estimate," Boyd said, speaking to someone at SAC. "we're attempting to get visual. well, we don't even know what it is, yet, sir. he's... on his way. yes, sir, as soon as he arrives. yessir. sir, one last question... is this a drill? i see. yessir. yessir, wilco." Boyd hung up the SAC phone, his fingers again white against it.

Walter raised an eyebrow at him.

"not a drill."

everyone paled. Boyd was motionless. David caught himself with his mouth open and pulled his dry lips tight together, hoping for moisture to come from somewhere.

Boyd took a breath and stood straight. "okay. it's not a drill. that's what it's not. we still don't know what it is. so everyone breathe. SAC is standing by, calling all their people in. i told them the Colonel was on his way. if we can't get him on the phone, we'll need to actually go and get him."

"what's their response?" Walter asked.

"they're going to scramble everything toward the coasts."

"everything?" David asked.

"everything," Boyd confirmed. "if it's nothing, they come back. if it's not nothing, they'll need every minute they have to reach and intercept the inevitable incoming Soviet wings."

"but... the coasts?" David asked.

"where else would they go?"

David looked at everyone else for their reaction. "well, ...here?"

Boyd stepped away from the phones to formally address those present. "men, if this threat is real and to the extent we expect, given the breach we're seeing play out, there aren't many realistic scenarios in which this building or this town survive. SAC is going to do what they can, but we have to play past that. we're not trying to save ourselves. we're trying to save the United States."

the fog of truth shrouded each man in his own thoughts.

"which means we also need to develop a contingency plan for SAC," Boyd continued. "once we're gone, they're going to need a backup way to communicate with everyone. Burke!"

Burke stood up, surprised. "sir?"

"quit sitting on your face and do something constructive. you're Communications, right?"

"yessir." some of the color returned to his face.

"you and Marston build a phone plan we can pass on to SAC."

"yessir." Burke, shaking, walked to Marston, and they cleared out a space on the end of the table to begin making notes.

David watched Leonard and Gordy, still taking calls coming in from around Colorado Springs. still laughing with the children. the children.

"the children, sir," David said, his throat calcifying.

"David," Boyd spoke, quiet as ever, firm as ever, but he sounded like a father. "all the children. from coast to coast."

David nodded, resolved.

there was a commotion up top as Mo and Pepper brought the short wave radio down from the cab, followed by Major McKellar and Captain Freeman.

Boyd put a hand on David's arm, getting his attention again. "SAC is sending squadrons from Malstrom, Mountain Home, and Ellsworth to roam the flight path you've laid out. that's good work. now let's see if we can fine tune it."

Pepper plugged in the radio and sat down at its controls. Mo yanked a wire from the back of his turntable, and quickly wired the PA speaker into the back of the short wave, giving him a small shock as he plugged it in.

"sorry bout that," Pepper said calmly. Mo sucked his finger as he returned to his spot on the floor. Roberts came over to inspect the speaker, realizing what it was.

"Bonner, what's this doing in here?"

"just trying to have a little fun, sir."

"you having fun now?"

"no, Major."

Roberts left it at that. for now.

"we were able to connect with RCAF," Captain Freeman said, "and we have an HF frequency for the pilots who think they've intercepted our 'blip'."

Major McKellar stepped up to the radio. "let's hope these canucks can outrun whatever this thing is."

Pepper turned up the volume, and Major McKellar grabbed the tabletop microphone.

"Osprey 3 1, this is Hawk. come in, over."

a squelch, and then, "this is Osprey 3 1, we read, over." the line was laden with static, as the radio waves fought their way down from way up north.

"emergency reserve frequencies have been relayed to you by the tower?"

"affirmative, Hawk."

"push frequency green zero niner, over."

"copy that. green zero niner. pushing frequency, over."

Pepper pulled a card from his binder. he scanned for the ninth on the green list and dialed in the radio.

"Hawk, this is Osprey 3 1, do you copy?"

"Osprey 3 1, Hawk. we copy." McKellar said. "from here, we'll push frequency by 30 Hz every three minutes," Pepper made notes on a scratch pad and started his stopwatch.

"roger that, Hawk."

"any visual on the contact?"

latent static crackled on the line like one of Mo's albums. no one breathed. "negative on a visual, Hawk, but i've got a pretty significant blip on the outer edge of my radar range. headed toward it now."

"what's the location, heading, speed... can you tell the size?"

"we are just westnorthwest of Brooks. course 110°, speed 650 miles per hour... contact is 9 miles out, course 170°, speed about 575 miles per hour at an altitude of 42,000 feet. we're closing in, hoping to come up in its wake."

David went to his chart for Alberta and adjusted his figures. then started calculating an accurate timeline. he was already zeroing in on correct minutes. eventually, it would be down to seconds. it made every moment of waiting through the radio silence feel like an hour.

"contact maintaining heading. contact..." the radio washed out, full of static.

David panicked. McKellar's eyes darted around at everyone else. he was panicked, too.

"come in, Osprey 3 1."

"three minutes," Pepper said quietly, showing his stopwatch.

"Osprey 3 1, do you read."

every crackle just made the ensuing silence that much emptier.

"sir, three minutes."

"i heard you, Tech Sergeant."

more waiting.

"okay, push frequency," McKellar relented.

Pepper dialed three clicks. "--mation maintaining the same heading. request guidance on how to proceed, over."

"Osprey 3 1, we're here now, but did not copy, please repeat your last transmission, over."

the pilot spoke distinctly and deliberately: "i say again, contact is actually single group, three contacts. three aircraft in vic formation. formation maintaining same heading as before. request guidance on how to proceed, over."

"we copy, Osprey, standby," McKellar released the talk button on the mic. "three planes. what the hell."

§

i saw three ships

"three planes?" Boyd repeated.

"sir," Roberts spoke up, "how is it any different than one in terms of our response?"

Boyd rubbed his temple. "well, it means it's not a passenger jet." David looked at Sollee. Sollee's shoulders fell.

"sir, how is it different--" Roberts pressed his question again.

Boyd nodded. "it's the same. how long to visual?"

McKellar relayed into the mic. "Osprey 3 1, proceed as directed. ETA to visual acquisition?"

"five minutes."

good grief, five minutes is going to feel like five days, David thought.

Boyd relaxed his tense posture. "everyone take a deep breath. can we get Major McKellar a chair?" Marston bolted up the stairs into the tiers.

Mo muttered under his breath as he lit a cigarette. "hundreds of thousands of dollars on a facility, multi-million dollar drill, and when the real thing happens, we're cobbling together a clubhouse on the pit floor with a wool map."

"Bonner, give it a rest," Roberts sighed. David was glad Roberts always said what everyone else was thinking. of course it didn't phase Mo one bit. Mo sat and took a drag, using his wastebasket as an ashtray. David laughed a little to himself, thankful for his friends' predictability.

his friends.

David looked around at each one of them.

Airman First Class Howard Alspach stood tall, listening. he was king of the den, and everyone loved him. Howard tried to make even the most boring paperwork evenings a great ride. David rarely went along for the ride. actually, he tended to be harsh with him. Howard had really taken him under his wing; even though he's only a few months older, he seemed years wiser. Howard was always trying to include him, and David always resisted. he respected and appreciated Howard, and it hurt when he realized he couldn't remember ever telling him.

in the tiers behind him, Airmen Leonard Cesana and George Gordy answered phones. they had the usual goofy expressions and were laughing with every phone call, blissfully ignorant of the war taking place on the pit floor. their antics were often annoying. but tonight, David could see they had the joy he wished he had. he didn't want to engage in everything they did, but they were able to have fun even when the work was hard, boring, or dire. David wished he had their same power to will joy into being. but he didn't.

Airman Bill Sollee sat on the stairs, watching everything from above, waiting for a command. he was a smart and thoughtful man. David hoped he would continue to advance well, but worried others might hold him back because of his skin color. David tried to think if he'd ever treated Bill different because of his skin color. David always felt like an outsider in this group, and he suddenly realized how Bill must feel. he was really glad Bill was here. and he'd never told him.

Technical Sergeant Dan "Pepper" Donaldson sat under him at the radio, watching his stopwatch. Pepper was kind and friendly, but David didn't know much about him. he was quiet. David considered all the thoughts he had going on in his own head. did everyone overthink everything like this? did Pepper have this many thoughts? if he did, he never voiced them. then again, David had never voiced most of his own thoughts. he and Pepper may have more in common than he realized. he might actually make a pretty good friend. if he could spend time with him. then he realized, maybe that's why Pepper came to sit with him at meals. trying to make a friend. David felt obtuse. "three minutes, pushing frequency," Pepper called calmly, and clicked the dial.

Marston placed a chair next to Major McKellar, who stood as stone, holding the tabletop microphone like a television field reporter. he was stern and commanded his space. how was he able to keep his work and home lives separate? David always took his stress home with him. home. home was the barracks. maybe David couldn't keep his home life separate because he didn't have one. he very much looked up to Major McKellar and wished he'd gotten to know him during those chapel times. but it was hard for David to not think of him as his superior officer.

Captain Bob Freeman flipped through a binder. he was always looking for solutions, even among the men. whenever there was an argument, he would play mediator, peacemaker. he didn't avoid confrontation, but wouldn't tolerate quarreling. and he was smart. he'd served in several countries and spoke all the languages there fluently. everyone was always amazed and wanted him to whip it out like a party trick, but for him, it was a matter of efficiency. speak the native language, and you can navigate the world you're in more quickly and get more done with the locals. David wanted to be this sharp and industrious, and hoped it was something that came with years of experience. David wasn't sure he'd have the chance, now. he thought of every unread book back in his barrack.

Major Pete Roberts still leaned on the first-tier desk, rubbing his chin. he was thinking. analyzing. he was so practical. David so frequently reacted from emotion or with the first idea that came into his head. Roberts parsed ideas, thought practically. David wished he could do that. he never crossed Roberts' path except in the Command Center when they were on duty, so he never got to know him personally. but he always treated David like a co-worker. they had their different positions in the hierarchy. but Roberts never treated him like a child. in turn, David realized he was a lot more relaxed when he had to assist Roberts with anything; he was a lot easier to work with. David felt like others found him difficult to work with, and now he wasn't sure if it was because they treated him like a child, or if they treated him that way because he was hard to work with. he wished he would work with everyone like he worked with Roberts. when he felt treated like a child, maybe he could remind himself that Roberts respected him.

Lieutenant Colonel James Boyd. Boyd was a giant. David did feel like a child around him, but not in a bad way. Boyd really took care of David. he was top dog on this shift, but even when he was number two or three, he always made sure David got good work that would challenge him. David wondered why he favored him. a question for another time. if there would be another time.

Marston and Burke continued to go through the directory, writing down numbers of bases. Walter was calling numbers and making notes on their pad. they had really gotten a system down, their arms dancing over each other. they were quiet, off to the side, but as the only noise in the room, everyone could now hear clearly every call Walter made. they were all short, which seemed like good news. Marston and Burke were crisply focused on their task. that was usual for Marston, but a bit surprising to in Burke. he seemed thankful for the distraction. even as lower-ranked airmen, it didn't take long to understand the critical work that was being done in the Command Center. but Burke was so new and green. David wished he'd done for Burke what Howard had done for him. if they made it out of this, he'd do it.

his gaze came full circle to Mo. Mo was dirty from re-wiring the guts of the Command Center. seated on the floor, he leaned back motionless against the wall next to the den, resting an elbow on that wastebasket. as David looked at his face, he saw Mo looking right at him. Mo had been watching him watch everyone else. Mo was funny, but he was angry. why was he angry. David always found Mo to be irritating. chaotic, crass, and brash. but here he stood. stoic. emotionless. quiet. with every drill, they taught David that people change when the moment really comes. so you have lean back on the training. the training has to be instinct. here in this short lull, David was seeing who Mo was when the moment came. he had given up. David wasn't irritated; he was sad.

at Mo's feet, David's bible. cover closed, lying in shadow.

David looked at his paper marker on the tapestry. he sketched out two more and tore them from his pad. he walked to the tapestry and pinned them in the vee-shaped vic formation along with the first.

"three minutes, pushing frequency," Pepper announced, and tuned the radio three more clicks.

"ah..." a hesitant voiced crackled over the radar a few seconds later. "okay, acquiring visual, Hawk, do you copy?"

"Osprey 3 1, this is Hawk. we copy. go ahead, over."

"three large aircraft. bombers. no fighters."

it was their worst fears confirmed. and of course there were no fighters. too far from home. everyone reacted as a ripple radiated from the radio to the tiers.

"what can you tell us about the aircraft," McKellar asked. *it could still be a drill*, David hoped.

"no lights. visibility up here... pretty clear, got a half moon. we're closing in. we'll spotlight 'em within one minute."

"any luck with radio communication?"

"negative, Hawk. Osprey 3 2's radioman has been around the horn. if they're hearing us, they're not responding."

a few more seconds passed, and the pilot's radio went live, but no one was speaking. just the sounds of cockpit. the pilot's slick flightsuit making noise as he shifted in his seat.

"okay Hawk we have visual. three bombers, vic formation." as the pilot talked, Boyd picked up the line to SAC. "pulling up alongside them. some glow in the cockpits from their instrument panels. Osprey 3 2," the pilot called over his short range radio to his wingman, "light 'em up."

Boyd had someone on the SAC line. "visual from RCAF is three incoming bombers, we presume Soviet... near Medicine Hat, Alberta... copy that, i have received an order to destroy all Soviet targets, please confirm." a tingle tightened all of David's skin and the hair on his neck shot up. this was the real thing.

"Hawk, Osprey 3 1, come in. we got-- eh-- standby."

standby? David looked around, everyone looked at each other. what was happening?

"okay, Hawk, we have visual on United States markings on all three aircraft."

every jaw dropped, from greenhorn to brass.

"can you repeat that, Osprey."

"wilco, Hawk. repeating, we have visual on what appears to be three B-29s, all with United States markings. these are yours, Major."

Boyd spoke quietly into the SAC line, "hang on, cancel that. there's been a change, standby." he pushed the handset to his chest. "do we have positive identification?" Boyd asked McKellar.

"he's says they're B-29s."

"the Soviet Tu-4 is an exact copy of the B-29," Roberts reminded them.

"i thought we were dealing with Tu-16s," Boyd said.

"we assumed that based on the ceiling, speed, and range," David said. "Tu-4 can't--"

"the Soviets are improving things all the time," Roberts said. "they could put Tu-16 power plants on the Tu-4--"

McKellar released the mic button. "jet engines on a prop plane?"

"they'd have the speed and range they need to get here, and they'd have the body they'd need for deception."

"they came across the arctic, they have to be Soviet," McKellar said. "we have the orders to take them down, right?"

"well, not now," Boyd said, "i just cancelled it with SAC. how sure are we they're Soviet? what's the possibility these are... reconnaissance planes... coming back from--"

"then why did they take off from Siberia?" Freeman asked.

"we don't know that they did," Roberts said. "the first thing we know is the blip over northern Canada."

"why would we be surveilling Canada?" Freeman said.

"it doesn't matter," Boyd said. "we report what we've heard to SAC and they make the call." Boyd spoke into the phone. "we have three incoming bombers with United States markings, please advise."

McKellar squeezed the mic button. "Osprey 3 1, do you see call numbers on the tail."

"ah... negative, Hawk, i don't see... tail appears to be freshly buffed.. wait a minute... we've got some numbers near the cockpit... looks like 82? could be Baker 2? 82? hard to tell."

"what about the other two?"

"hard to see, but... looks like they might also be 82?"

McKellar released the mic button and shook his head. "three bombers with the same number?"

"guys, for whatever it's worth, the Enola Gay was numbered 82."

"Enola Gay is in storage at Andrews in Maryland," Sollee said.

"my point is," Roberts continued, "there's few bombers that have had hundreds of pictures taken of it. if they're trying to copy US markings, they're probably looking at a photograph of the Enola Gay."

McKellar looked at Boyd. "they have to be Soviet."

Boyd took a deep breath and lifted the handset. "okay so visual is: single group, three aircraft, appear to be B-29s with US markings, but might be Tupolev Tu-4s in disguise. do you have any information?" everyone waited while Boyd listened. "it's not a secret mission of some kind? recon planes or a refueling--" Boyd waited and then rolled his eyes, dropping the handset again. he looked at McKellar. "their top people still aren't there yet."

"where are they?" David didn't realize he'd said it out loud until Boyd glared at him.

"they're at home, airman. it's Christmas Eve."

"three minutes, pushing frequency," Pepper announced, and advanced the dial three clicks.

"still, someone there would know about it if they were ours," McKellar cut in.

"they can't give the order to take down three aircraft if there's a chance they're American," Boyd continued, "they want a hundred-percent confirmation from LeMay or Griswold before they give take-down orders. they're on their way in. few minutes away. and they're scrambling squads from Malstrom and Ellsworth just in case."

"we don't have a few minutes," McKellar said, with force.

"actually, yes. we do have a *few* minutes," Boyd said.

"do you want us to try the Colonel again, sir?" Walter asked. Boyd nodded, and Walter lifted the handset and dialed. he looked at Boyd and shook his head.

"keep trying," Boyd said, then looked around. "where's Gordy?"

Howard spoke up from the fringe of the huddle. "he's on the phones, sir."

Boyd turned to find Howard. "okay, well, get an airman over to the Colonel's house."

Howard snapped at Marston. "get directions from Gordy and take my truck. it's over by the barracks." he tossed him his keys.

"Hawk, Osprey 3 1 awaiting instructions." the voice on the radio sounded nervous. that made David nervous.

McKellar huffed into the mic. "we know. we're looking into something. standby."

"uh.. yes sir. copy that. just... we spotlighted 'em. we kinda got our zipper open here, if you know what i mean."

McKellar looked at Boyd. Boyd shrugged hard. "i don't have a directive from SAC yet."

McKellar mashed the button on the mic. "Osprey 3 1, we do not have confirmation of any of our aircraft in your airspace. we believe the markings to be false, and we believe these are Soviet bombers. but we are waiting for a directive from Strategic Air Command on whether or not to down the craft."

"copy that, Major, but i'm going to need a verified command from my own superior before i shoot down an airplane with a USAF star on it, sir."

McKellar lowered the mic and laughed nervously. "come on. they're obviously Soviet with fake markings. we shoot them down."

"i'm with you, Ed, but it's not our call. and these guys aren't our airmen." Boyd stared him down. McKellar was in disbelief. David watched them both. it was a tough position to be in, and they were both right. it was clearly a misdirection, and it wasn't our call to give orders, certainly not to another sovereign nation's air force. David looked at his charts and checked his timeline.

"sir, five minutes to American airspace," David announced.

McKellar nodded, "then, it's our problem." *it's a double-edged sword*, David thought. *it will be entirely our control, but entirely our responsibility* — and less than an hour from Colorado Springs.

"Hawk this is Osprey 3 1... we've got a light on. nearest aircraft, right side-- Osprey 3 2! right side!" the shout from the radio startled the whole room, and the radio went dead quiet.

McKellar frantically strangled the microphone. "Osprey 3 1, come in. what's going on?" no answer. "Osprey!"

the radio cut in and blasts of pops could be heard. it wasn't static. David recognized that sound from his Uncle P. B.'s stories. they were being shot at. "Hawk, we are being fired upon. we managed to evade, but Osprey 3 2 is hit, and they ejected. repeat, Osprey 3 2 is down." everyone sat up and leaned forward. David shifted his tugged at his starched collar. there was no question what this was now.

Boyd was already in his handset to SAC. "they just fired upon two Royal Canadian Air Force Sabres. one friendly down, the men ejected. remaining friendly evaded and is awaiting instructions." Boyd listened intently on the phone. he looked at McKellar and nodded. "i have received an order to take down all three aircraft, is that confirmed." Boyd waited. "i have your confirmation. we will relay the orders to RCAF now."

McKellar started speaking before Boyd finished. "Osprey 3 1, Hawk. we have orders from Strategic Air Command to take down all three bombers. repeat, take them all down."

"one Sabre against three bombers?" Roberts said.

"Osprey 3 1, returning fire."

McKellar rolled his eyes. "don't need RCAF orders now, do they."

"no," Roberts said, "but they're going to need backup."

Boyd covered his handset as he jotted notes on a nearby pad. "SAC is on the line with RCAF. we're working on it. Malstrom and Ellsworth are already in the air." David went to his maps and started marking out possible flight paths from Malstrom AFB in Montana and Ellsworth AFB in South Dakota.

"maneuver! formation breaking up, rightmost bomber slowing down--" a series of pops and the Canadian engine revved as his plane swooped to dodge the enemy fire. "they're firing on us... falling back!"

"three minutes! pushing frequency," Pepper called out and reached for the knob. McKellar grabbed his wrist.

"wait a minute, dammit."

the popping stopped and the Sabre's engine noise leveled out. "bomber returning to formation. they are on a mission!"

his engine revved once more, and the spatter of firefight returned. the Sabre shot back, loud blasts distorting the small speaker. suddenly it went dead.

"Osprey 3 1, come in."

Pepper looked up at McKellar, who still clutched his wrist. "sir, push frequency." McKellar shook the fog from his head and let go of Pepper's wrist. three clicks and the radio was back in action.

"i tagged a wing, he's leaking--" a few pops then BOOM! and the engine noise revved high and the tone dropped low. "we're hit! mayday, mayday, mayday!"

David watched as McKellar stood there with the mic in his hand, powerless. Boyd stared at the radio, the black SAC phone pressed to his ear.

"my pilot is out."

McKellar closed his eyes.

"electrical is out. eject's not working."

"manual release..." McKellar said to himself, eyes still closed.

"pulling manual release--" and a great rush of noise blanched the radio. another FOOM and the co-pilot's eject was gone, leaving the radio behind, killing the audio instantly. the radio was silent, save a light dusting of crackle.

McKellar set the mic down.

Boyd spoke somberly into the SAC handset. "all friendlies down. mission failed."

§

checking it twice

Major Tilday opened the cab with a whoosh and looked down where everyone in the pit stood disheartened.

"sir?"

"standby, Colonel." Boyd set down the black handset and turned, acknowledging Tilday.

"there's activity in Soviet coastal airbases," the Major said. "we've got several recon planes reporting back to their carriers. nothing is airborne yet, but every Russian runway we have eyes on is lined up with bombers."

"thank you, Major. keep the calls going out. we need all the intel we can."

"yes, sir," Tilday said, disappearing back into the cab.

Boyd spoke back into the black phone. "sir, we're getting reports of Soviet air and navy activity. no sir, nothing in the air yet, but we'll keep you updated. well. that's a good question. yes, sir. yes, sir. i understand. yes, sir, standby." Boyd addressed everyone on the floor. "okay, we need to create a backup communications plan. if they wipe us out, they could do a full US strike within a few hours. if we wait any longer, we won't have time to get a communication contingency plan in place."

"well, they're not gonna wipe us out, because we're going to blow these planes out of the sky, right?" McKellar said, his face turning pink.

"SAC has sent one ready squadron from Malstrom--"

"one??" McKellar exploded.

"why does Malstrom only have one squadron?" Freeman asked.

"they have eight, with only three ready to fly. but this is the beginning of war. the rest have been directed to escort the bombers leaving Fairchild AFB in Spokane."

McKellar shook his head, seemingly unable to even speak. David had never seen him so furious.

"how many bombers are flying out of Fairchild?" Freeman asked.

"every one they have a crew for." Boyd looked at his notes. "Mountain Home in Idaho is also sending out every bomber they have. even so, they spared us a fighter squadron, however, the timeline is tight for them to intercept." David looked at his charts. very tight. "Ellsworth is sending two squadrons. they're on their way to the coast anyway. and Wendover is sending one, if they can make it in time. the rest of theirs are escorting bombers west. there's one fighter squadron on standby from Naval Air Station Denver--"

"how do *they* have only one fighter squadron?" McKellar asked, gaining a little composure. "i know they don't have bombers to escort."

"it's an inland Navy Reserve base. and it's Christmas. it doesn't matter. Naval Air Station Denver is a last resort, and we'll supplement with whatever we have ready here over at Pete Field.

we shouldn't even need any of that. the Ellsworth squadrons should be enough to take care of business."

"what about Lowry?" Roberts asked.

"Lowry is mostly cadets," Boyd said.

"and bombers," added McKellar.

"right, which are all going to the coasts. they need what few squadrons they have at the ready to escort their bombers."

"so that's it?" McKellar said, still purple.

"those are the only air bases along the heading with time enough to be in range," Boyd said, "and it ought to be plenty. everything else — and i do mean everything — is being directed either to the coasts, to protection zones, or into enemy airspace. based on what the men in the cab are giving us, that's warranted. this is exactly the plan from Crackerjack. and i again remind you, SAC is playing past whatever happens here."

"this attack is different than the Crackerjack drill," Roberts said.

"okay," Captain Freeman said, trying to calm the tension, "so that's, what..." he counted on his fingers. "... 72 fighters against three unescorted bombers. with... 48 backups that may or may not make it in time." he said it as if it spoke for itself, but David didn't know if 72 fighters could take down three Soviet bombers. he'd not been in combat. it seemed like good odds. but as he looked around at the other officers, they didn't seem confident either.

"SAC wants a tight, clear course heading and timeline," Boyd said.

"Michaels." with the mention of his name, he suddenly remembered he was part of this, not watching on television. he looked toward the sound. it was Mo. "don't you have something to do?" somehow he was still able to stare down his nose at him, even from sitting on the floor.

"yes, sergeant." embarrassed, David clambered for his pens. his hands were trembling. he tried to breathe deeply. *rely on the training*, he told himself. he checked his measurements. "1 minute until US airspace." now that they had more exact data, Michaels started mapping it out on his paper charts. he looked up at the giant plexiglass maps, his Santa artwork dipping down into the midwest. "guess we can use these now," he said to himself. he grabbed a roll of charts, then headed off behind the mapboards.

"sir," Walter approached him with his pad. "i think we have a contingency plan that can put SAC in direct communication with the major coastal bases. each of them are quickly establishing an ad hoc command center to process what they know from nearby Naval carriers, other air bases closest to them, and Ground Observer Corp intel, then pass the pertinents along to SAC."

"thank you, Lieutenant. i'll connect you with SAC." Boyd picked up the black phone. "sir? yes i'm handing you off to 2nd Lieutenant Walter Gamble. he'll let you know what our contingency plan is in case we're neutralized."

"neutralized," Mo repeated, still sitting against the wall.

Boyd handed off the phone to Walter. "Airman Sollee, get the Malstrom tower on the line." and Sollee went to work.

David grabbed his cleaning spray and a rag. he sprayed the bottom part of his artwork and pressed hard, clearing away the grease pencil markings. everyone on the pit floor watched as David erased "Merry Christmas!!".

"well that's a pisser," Howard said.

"sorry, guys, i need the map." David unrolled his charts on the floor and began making red marks on the mapboards, indicating the plane's trajectory, writing the times at key intervals. in blue, he marked dashed lines for the squadrons from Malstrom, Mountain Home, Ellsworth, and Wendover, guessing at their trajectories.

Sollee handed Boyd the green phone. he watched David calculate and make his marks. with a few seconds, David was done and stepped back to look at it. he checked his watch and spoke to the others through the glass. "sir, contact is now in US airspace."

"you're ours now, bastards," McKellar grunted.

"this is Boyd. you have a radio in the air for us?"

Walter pulled back the SAC receiver against his shoulder. "sir, SAC is going to get a party line going with SAC, us, the major bases on our list, and the Pentagon."

"and the White House?" until everyone's head snapped his way, David didn't even realize he'd said it out loud. they stared at him through the glass like he were an exhibit at the zoo.

"why, what's the point?" Boyd asked, as if the answer was obvious. his brow stabbed at him for interrupting.

"well, sir... he's the Commander in Chief."

everyone rolled their eyes.

"he asks *us* what to do," said Boyd.

Mo growled at David under his breath. "if we get blown up, we'll inform him first thing in the morning."

Boyd spoke, firmly, loudly. "QUIET." a second, rare appearance of his raised tone silenced the room. Boyd was hunched over a slip of paper, writing, the green phone tucked into his neck. "got it. standby." he tossed the green handset to Sollee and handed the slip to Pepper, who immediately started adjusting the shortwave radio.

"--mmand, come in, do you read. over."

McKellar picked up the mic again. "Malstrom, this is CONAD Command, we read you, over."

"awaiting emergency reserve frequency orders, over."

McKellar bent over Pepper's shoulder. Pepper held up his card. "push frequency green zero four."

"copy that." and the line went dead. Pepper adjusted the frequency of the shortwave, and the line was live again. "CONAD Command, this is Technical Sergeant Henry Sprott with the 29th Fighter Interceptor Squadron out of Malstrom Air Force Base. do you read?"

"affirmative, Tech Sergeant."

"we are on a course of 62° and expect to acquire target at 2104." David looked at his watch. three minutes.

"roger that, Tech Sergeant."

Boyd was on the green phone again. "the 54th out of Ellsworth is on track to intercept near Billings if this gets through the Malstrom squadron."

"don't count on it," said McKellar. "24 fighters against three shoddy Soviet bombers?" he pressed the mic button. " Tech Sergeant, we are assigning your squadron Red designation, Red 1 1 through 4 6."

"copy that, CONAD, but there's only 16 of us."

McKellar dropped the mic to his waist. "what the hell."

"they sent what was ready," Boyd said, a calm boil.

"they can't rustle men out of their bunks and into the cockpit?"

"they had three squadrons at the ready," Boyd explained, taking the SAC phone back from Walter. "they sent two to the coast and one here. they'll man the rest of their squadrons asap, but not in time to be of any use to us--" a voice in Boyd's receiver interrupted him, and he plugged his free ear. "hello, yes this is Boyd again. do you have squadron headings for us?" he listened and jotted down a note. he tore it out of his small spiral pad, then began writing on the next sheet. "just double checking, that's 14,

16, 14, and 12." a silence while he shook his head. "copy that. standby."

Pepper held up his stopwatch to McKellar. McKellar spoke into the mic. "we'll push frequency 30 Hz every three minutes. starting now." Pepper started the timer spinning.

"copy that, CONAD."

Boyd laid the phone down, tore the second note, and handed one to Sollee. "give this to Michaels."

"yes, sir." Sollee ran to the back of the mapboards and handed the note to David.

Boyd handed the other note to Pepper. "call signs for the incoming squadrons." Pepper looked it over. "Mountain Home is sending their fighters to meet up with Ellsworth near Billings," Boyd announced, as David looked over his note. "Wendover and Naval Air Station Denver are going to intercept near Casper as a last line of defense."

David's note was the numbers of planes with times to intercept the heading. from Mountain Home in Idaho, 14 fighters that may not make it. from Ellsworth fighter squadrons of 16 and 14, and from Wendover only 12 fighters who were going to be cutting it really close. 72 fighters with 48 maybes dropped to 46 and 26 real fast. the bombers were still outnumbered 15 to 1. but then, this wasn't all at the same time. 16 fighters on this first attack... that's only 5 to 1. still seemed like an upper hand. wasn't it?

David checked his watch and updated the mapboard. he marked the number of planes, watching Major McKellar as he did it. he could see him doing the calculations with every new figure. McKellar said nothing just shook his head.

Boyd answered McKellar, as if hearing his thoughts. "everyone's on minimal staff for the holiday. Mo, can you get the SAC party line connected to your speaker there?"

Mo didn't say a word, just got up and walked into the utility room. he wanted Mo to have a smart aleck remark. or to point out that they had all this functionality in the cab, until he was asked to start dismantling things. but he said nothing. just worked silently. David hurt for him; that was a new feeling. Mo exited the utility room with a small box and a handful of wires. in a minute, he had the shortwave and the SAC phone coming through the PA speaker.

"it's live," Mo said. "you'll still have to use the handset to talk, though."

Boyd set the handset on top of the shortwave on the table in front of him. "can you read me, Colonel?"

"loud and clear," a stern, official voice on the other end said. there was a light ring of feedback. Mo turned the speaker away from the handset, and it stopped. he walked back to his spot against the tier wall and slid back down to the floor.

"come in, CONAD." it was easy to tell the young pilots from the older brass, even through the tinny PA speaker. "we have visual on the target."

"we read you, Red 1 1," McKellar replied. "you're our eyes in the air, so get a good position and stay out of the fray. and stay sharp. they'll be expecting you."

§

white Christmas

"copy that, CONAD."

he had barely stopped speaking when faint pops could be heard, and the air battle commenced.

"they didn't even hesitate!" the radioman narrated everything in real time. "as soon as we were in range, they were all over us. these things are armed to the teeth. holy cow, they got one already, plane down!" that's 15, David counted. "that was fast. they are raining fire on us."

everyone could hear the pops in the background, a steady stream from both sides.

"we're giving it right back to them. sparks are flying off their fuselage... they must have these things armored up."

that didn't make sense to David. to get even a modified Tu-4 past its maximum range, it'd have to be empty, essentially a flying gas can. the extra plating would add a lot of weight. that combined with being full of bombs... unless they weren't full of bombs. three planes full of bombs wouldn't be needed to take out CONAD. Boyd was right. it really amounted to one three-story building. even the smallest nuclear weapon would take out the entire Ent Air Force Base, all of CONAD, and most of Colorado Springs. these planes didn't have lots of bombs. they probably had one. and a lot of armor.

"three more down. they've got machine guns added all over these things. they've got some kind of heavy gun mounted into the bubbles-- another one! hit us again!" one boom, then another. "explosion sent one of our fighters into pieces, downing two more... i see.. two parachutes... maybe i missed the others.. i hope to God..."

and like that, they were down to twelve. David updated his board. the men on the pit floor listened helplessly.

"these turrets are doing some damage. they're on top on bottom, rear gunners front gunners side gunners, these things are lit up like a roman candle with all the muzzle flashes. we got two of our Sabres smoking... they can't keep up, looks like they've fallen back and headed for an emergency landing."

ten. things were going down quickly.

"two Sabers approaching their six. turrets spinning. sparks flying off the wings. we're aiming for the fuel tanks in the wings and, just, nothing. turrets coming around!"

another loud series of pops. David knew what that meant. eight left.

"two on the six are down," the radioman confirmed. "we've got two for each bomber going head on. circling around. here they come. right into a wall of fire. one down. glass shattering on the bomber cockpits.. bombers still on course. i think they've even double- or triple-paned the windows. one more down! dammit!"

more pops, loud whooshes.

"four of ours survived the front-on.. they're circling around for another pass. we've got one crossing over laterally, aiming for the gunmen in the open bubbles, fuel tanks in the wings... no significant damage there yet. and we're trying to stay back to report, but we're going to have to square up soon. here come the four from the front again. bomber turrets are full front. bullets everywhere, like a shield of fire."

a series of loud pings indicated the radioman's plane wasn't that far out of range.

"we're getting hit, we're not even in the action. from the front... one fighter is smoking... another going down! men ejected... okay, i think i see a small explosion in one of the bomber cockpits, maybe the windows shattering? looks like we finally broke through... bomber is sinking... wait.. it's coming back into formation. there's a new pilot in the cockpit.. everyone has a gas mask or something... cabin must be depressurized.. these guys are prepared. how many-- HOLY-- they just tossed a body out the side... holy shit."

"godless sons of bitches," McKellar said, to no one in particular.

"smoking fighter trailing off... i don't think they'll keep up. we're going in. joining the remaining two fighters for another frontal attack. lateral plane joining us as well."

the engines groaned loudly as the last four planes veered around to face the bombers.

"coming in fast and firing!" the radioman grunted out his play by play as his pilot pushed them into the fight. lots of loud pops as the US fighters pelted the oncoming bombers. "bombers shifting position, hard to stay locked on, rotating like they're juggling... these are top pilots and their gunners are locked on us."

more pops and two loud booms.

"just lost both our wingmen."

a loud whoosh and the last two fighters were past the bombers.

"two of us left... the other is... got an engine on fire, but still circling around. turrets coming around!"

a few loud pops and a short screech of static and the line went dead.

McKellar slammed the mic down hard onto the table.

"Boyd," came the stern voice from SAC, "it was a little hard for us to hear clearly... are any of our fighters still in play?"

"negative."

"and the bombers?"

"sounds like all three are still alive, well, and on target. Michaels, how long until Ellsworth and Wendover hit the heading?" Boyd asked.

David was scrawling figures on paper and transferring his corrected times to the back of the plexiglass. "less than eight minutes, sir."

"okay what have we learned so far?" Boyd asked the room.

no one answered.

it was clear to David. these were some of the Soviet's best pilots. they were well trained for these exact kind of attacks. they'd rehearsed this. and they knew they were going to die when they took off from northern Siberia. they are on a serious mission and intend to reach their destination. the only reason to commit your best people to a suicide mission was if it were only the beginning of something much larger. and based on the way this was going, the ensuing bi-coastal air assault was going to be a slaughter. but he certainly wasn't going to be the one to point it out. he looked around at everyone else, and their faces said they already knew.

"okay, let's try it another way. how would we take down a B-29?"

"superfortress?" Roberts added.

"they're not invincible. they've been downed."

"not many," Roberts said.

"coming at the front," McKellar said. "taking out the pilots. but these guys have layered up on the bulletproof glass in the cockpit and seem to have a line of pilots waiting to die."

"it's not an endless line," Captain Freeman said. "so we just keep coming at them from the front? we've already breached one of the cockpits. maybe the others are close to breaking."

"so if we just keep firing down the nose--" McKellar said, nodding.

Boyd was nodding, too. "Lieutenant Gamble, get us a pilot with the 54th out of Ellsworth."

"yessir!" and Walter was on the green phone.

Roberts walked around the rail and came down the stairs, finally stepping onto the pit floor. "Ellsworth is sending... how many?"

Howard looked at David's markings. "16 and 14... 30 fighters."

"okay, 30... that's 10 fighters for each bomber."

"surely, 30 fighters can take down these bombers," McKellar said, unsure.

"plus the 12 from Wendover," David reminded them.

"are they going to make it?" Roberts asked, walking to the map.

David measured and re-checked his numbers. "they won't intercept until near Casper."

"and Mountain Home?"

David measured and calculated. "at this point... if they're really burning through fuel and the squadrons from Ellsworth can slow the bombers down some. otherwise..."

"14 fighters from Mountain Home, in or out?" Roberts pressed.

David held up his hands, unwilling to commit.

"don't count them out," Boyd said. "but it's clear they'll at least be delayed. that's still 42 fighters total, even without them."

"i'd feel a lot better if all 42 were going to arrive at the same time," McKellar said. "the 12 from Wendover are going to be batting clean up, looks like. and the group from Mountain Home may be on a fool's errand."

"even so, that's still 10 fighters per bomber with just the two squadrons from Ellsworth," Captain Freeman said. "surely that will be enough."

"they just ripped through 16 fighters with minimal damage," McKellar said, as if the whole room hadn't been there minutes ago listening to the carnage.

"but still damage," Freeman said.

"they didn't even slow down," McKellar said, his temper flaring again.

"not quite," Roberts said calmly. "at least one of the bombers did slow down, according to the radioman's report." *that's true*, David thought. "and damage is cumulative. every pass, we take a little more off. if we keep at it, keep coming at the front."

McKellar sighed. David sensed he wasn't frustrated with Roberts, rather frustrated that he was right. and this meant losing more fighters. and more pilots.

Boyd looked around the room. no one protested. "Colonel?"

"yes?"

"we're not sure what SAC wants to do, but we're recommending single-file trail formation attacks on a single bomber until it goes down. then the same on bombers two and three until all three bombers are down, or our resources are depleted."

David imagined the fighters running out of ammo, then he realized Boyd probably meant the planes. and pilots.

"roger. standby."

the few seconds of waiting that followed felt like an hour. David could hear the murmur of voices from the other end of the line. the room full of officers at SAC were no doubt having the same kind of conversations they'd had at CONAD all night. David couldn't stop thinking about those pilots floating in the dark over Montana ranches. how would they get home?

"the consensus here," finally came the reply, "is that CONAD has the best position to make that call based on what you just heard. so we're in agreement here. Generals will be in soon and may have further input. if you'll get your next radioman from Ellsworth on your end, we'll get in touch with Wendover, Mountain Home, and Naval Air Station Denver and get instructions to their people."

"roger, wilco," Boyd said, then whispered to Pepper. "get online with Ellsworth, asap."

"on it, sir," said Pepper. he cradled the green handset to his shoulder as Walter dialed another number in his directory.

"SAC, until we get them on the radio, we're on standby," Boyd said into the mic.

"roger that, CONAD."

Boyd took a deep breath, then stepped away from the makeshift battlestation on the pit floor. he walked up into the tiers and sat next to Gordy.

"what color of dress do you think she would like?" Gordy said into the phone, eyeing Boyd nervously.

Boyd waited, staring at the telephone in front of him.

"sir, what are you doing?" McKellar asked.

"gentlemen. we have one job: let America sleep in peace. and there are two parts to that job. one is destroying those enemy bombers. but the other is making sure our children don't grow up in fear of an unseen enemy. so we will do whatever we can about those bombers. but there's nothing happening for the next.." Boyd checked his watch. "...five minutes. so i'm going to answer a phone call or two." the telephone in front of him rang. he snapped it up.

Captain Freeman stepped up into the tiers and sat at a phone also. the others on the pit floor watched.

Mo paced a short, fast path. "this is stupid."

"he's just trying to comfort the children, Mo," David said.

"the children? what about us?" Mo pulled a cigarette from his pocket and lit it, taking a long drag.

"he has his way of staying calm and you have yours--"

"blow it out your ass, Michaels." Mo retraced his tight little path over and over, sucking on his cigarette, barely breathing between drags.

David watched that cigarette and hoped he sucked it into his throat. maybe it would catch his whole head on fire.

Mo burned his cigarette to the filter, then dropped it and smashed it into the concrete floor with the toe of his black loafer. "well Michaels, looks like you might get that white Christmas after all. of course, it's a nuclear winter, so you'll only have a second or two to enjoy it."

heat burst from every pore in David's face. Mo walked off, headed into the tunnel. David followed him.

Mo opened the door to the bathroom, and David chased him in, surprising him.

"do you mind?"

"yeah, sarge. i mind. i'm tired of your constant picking on me."

"you're tired of getting 'picked on'?" Mo started boiling. "are you kidding me? you're Boyd's little pet. you got your own 'team'. you're the chief voice on the floor. you've got the important work. i'm a Technical Sergeant. i outrank you. i should be the top dog on the floor, but Boyd has me running around like his monkey boy--"

"the whole reason you're even working tonight is because you mouthed off--"

"i know what i did. i don't need it thrown back at me from some busybody airman. and what about Pepper? hell, Michaels, you're not even first on the airman list. Howard has a couple of months on you. he's been standing back all night with his thumb up his ass."

David thought about it. Howard hadn't done much. he'd been standing there waiting, assisting David. Mo was right. it should have been the other way around.

"so i don't want to hear about being picked on. everyone picks on me all the time. you don't see me cryin about it."

"because you ask for it, with your attitude." David shot back.

"and you don't?" Mo said, as if it should be obvious. it wasn't obvious to David. what did that mean? the only thing Mo was a victim of was his own mouth. he made his own life difficult. that wasn't the case with David... was it?

"i'd rather have that idiot Burke getting the applause than you."

"Burke wouldn't have had a problem if you hadn't taken the speaker down in the den. you're the whole reason we're in a panic right now!"

"YOU THINK I DON'T KNOW THAT???" Mo's shouting scared David, and he flinched and backed away. Mo slowly recoiled, his face tense, his eyes red and wet. "i know. i know what i did."

David had never seen Mo express remorse of any kind. Mo looked as if he might weep. suddenly he erected himself, took in a deep breath and held it. he glared at David, and exited the bathroom.

David's blood thumped in his neck. his shallow breathing deepened. he went to the sink and splashed cold water on his face. remembering, he checked his watch and hurried back out to the pit.

§

the stars in the sky looked down

the radioman from Ellsworth was already on the radio as David re-entered the pit floor. Boyd and Freeman were back near the radio where McKellar was seated next to Pepper.

"got fifteen in front of us in a combat box formation. we're hanging way back and low so i have a good visual. the three bombers are up ahead of us. we should have visual any second."

everyone in the command center held their breath, waiting. except for Gordy and Leonard who kept answering calls from the children. it was about a quarter after nine. the youngest children had no doubt been shuffled off to bed, but calls kept coming in. the only sounds in the Command Center were the crackling shortwave and the ringing phones.

"there's only sixteen?" David whispered to Howard. "what about the other squadron?"

"they're about five minutes behind them."

"what?"

"yeah, McKellar was pissed."

David got back behind his map and noted the current locations of the two squadrons, now separated by five minutes. it had taken the three bombers six minutes to eliminate all sixteen fighters from Malstrom. maybe the second squadron would get there before the first fighters from Ellsworth were toast.

the radio squelched in, breaking the silence. "we see 'em. Blue Squad is falling out into trail formation and pouring it to it. here we go!" engines revving and the crackle of pops could be heard, even over the loud cockpit noise. it grew louder and suddenly quieter. "okay we've made the first pass. pulling back around so we can watch from behind the bombers... gonna stay low, avoid the friendly fire..."

the silences between transmissions punctuated the tension.

"okay, we can see Blue Squad curling around for another pass... two, four... ten... i only count thirteen. got two birds MIA."

McKellar sighed.

"they're coming back for a run on the western bomber, their left, our right. right-most bomber. maneuver! looks like Ruskies have wised up, they're adjusting formation."

David was rapt, his grease pencil in hand. he checked his watch, and made a mark on the bomber's path, moving them a little closer to Colorado Springs.

"okay, center bomber has fallen back... bombers are now in an inverted vic."

"they're protecting the middle one," Freeman said. McKellar nodded. David studied his face; he had just been listening before, and now he was listening for something.

"Blue Squad coming back... just enough space between them so they don't take each other out... holy shit! there must be ten or twelve gunneries on each bomber. first Sabre down. second one blasting away, flame out, peeling away smoking... Blue 2 3 chugging away, passing by, sparks flying off his belly. they can't get away from them. Blue 3 1 and 3 2 over, veering off different directions... we'll keep 'em guessing... damn! Blue 3 3 down."

the Russians were well trained and very smart. but it's hard to prepare any military in the world for American ingenuity. it had been the lynchpin in every major U.S. victory since Concord and Lexington. even so, they were up against the Soviets' bloodthirsty, brute strength.

"next three made a pass and are safe away. four more... hang on... maneuver! center bomber is dropping way back... coming low--" a barrage of pops and pings punched through the speaker. "shit! they're not falling back, they're coming after us!" more pops, then the radio was overcome with white noise. the radioman was yelling over the noise, but it was unintelligible. then it went dead silent.

"shit!" everything on the table jumped as McKellar slammed his fist down.

Boyd was as still and focused as ever. "get me the tower in Billings, we need to get through to another--"

"we've got another radio here, sir," Pepper said calmly. he was dialing in the radio. "we got three when we called Ellsworth."

"good man, Donaldson," Boyd said, putting a hand on Pepper's shoulder. Pepper nodded to McKellar.

"Blue 4 1, this is Hawk. come in. do you read? over."

silence.

"i say again, Blue 4 1, this is Hawk, do you read, over."

nothing. everyone knew what that meant.

"double-check your frequency, Tech Sergeant," McKellar said anyway. and Pepper checked it again anyway, then shook his head.

"okay. maybe the third one is still hot." *alive, you mean*, David thought.

Pepper dialed in the radio, then nodded to McKellar.

"Blue 5 3, this is Hawk, do you read? over."

silence.

Roberts sighed loudly.

then...

"roger, Hawk, this is Blue 5 3, over."

everyone breathed.

"we've lost our eyes up there. pull away to a vantage point so you can tell us what the hell is going on."

"wilco, Colonel."

Major McKellar didn't correct him.

"okay we're in their six and low. besides us, there's seven Sabres left fighting."

everyone's posture changed with the disappointment. David changed his figures on the mapboard. another minute or so and the second squad would be there.

"they'll see you down there from the rear gunner station, so keep your distance," McKellar said.

"copy that, Colonel."

David watched the second hand on his watch. "next squadron arrives in less than 60 seconds."

"Blue Squad making a second approach. they're coming in one line high, one line low. first two are up, in range, blasting away. shredded! bombers just ripped through them like tin foil. they were totally expecting it. next pair are weaving.. i think.. i think i see sparks on the cockpit."

"you can see the cockpit?" McKellar asked.

the radio stayed silent.

"Blue Squad, can you see the cockpit, over," he repeated.

"sorry, Hawk, yes. when you advised earlier, we pulled out to about four o'clock. last three fighters coming in, box. all three opening fire. i think they've broken through the cockpit... yes, bomber one is sinking!"

"yes!" McKellar said through clenched teeth.

"Blue Squad coming back to work on the next one-- wait a minute... no... i don't... bomber one is pulling back up, pushing back up into formation."

McKellar released his clench and leaned back in his chair, face toward the ceiling, eyes shut.

"five birds of Blue Squad coming back around, they're going after the eastern bomber now."

"no," McKellar shouted, smashing the mic button down. "finish off the first one."

"copy that, standby." and the radio went silent. he was back in a few seconds. "okay first three making a pass at bomber 2, only the last two were able to pull back toward bomber 1. bomber 1 is still plugging away unphased. and here comes the cavalry. fourteen Thunderstreaks all in a row. comin across at a forty-five, firing. whoa!"

everyone leaned toward the PA speaker.

"okay, we've pulled way out. we were right in their line of fire. good grief, there's planes everywhere. they're coming together, circling back for another pass. all three bombers still steady."

"still steady," Captain Freeman said, incredulous.

"lightin 'em up like a string of Christmas lights." David could hear a barrage of gunfire so dense it sounded like frying bacon. "ooh! a few of ours are out of commission.. i see a couple of chutes... EXPLOSION IN THE COCKPIT!"

McKellar jumped up, even Roberts stood up straight. David came around to the front of the maps. explosion? cockpit? whose cockpit?

"bomber one is going down!" a small eruption of cheers broke out on the floor." they're still shooting from every gunnery as they're sinking."

"hard-headed bastards," McKellar said, smiling.

"everyone, settle," Boyd yelled, "we have two of these left."

"Blue 5 3, can you get us a count of our remaining aircraft?"

"wilco, Hawk. standby."

Roberts was pacing, the most movement he'd displayed all night.

"okay i count twelve total besides us, mix of 86s and 84s." Sabres and Thunderstreaks. David ran back behind the map and updated his chart. he got a lot of pleasure out of wiping one of the bombers off the board. "next pass, coming through on the eastern bomber--"

"negative, go for the center bomber!" McKellar urged.

"eh.. there's only two now, there is no center."

McKellar tried to choke the stupid out him through the mic. "no, the one that WAS the center."

"sorry, Hawk, the bombers are doing their own maneuvers up here with us, i'm not sure which was which any more-- two safely by! next pair coming through..."

a loud jostling shook the PA speaker.

"hitting an air pocket. bombers must be going through it, too, they're wigglin... HOLY moses, two 84s just smashed into each other, God help us."

the turbulence caused a few more loud bangs.

"hold steady, pilot. two more 86s down!" said the Ellsworth radioman. "i see chutes though. damn. and our last pair passing by, i think we got some glass on that one."

"last pair?" Freeman said "that only makes six."

"was that six or eight?" Roberts asked.

"we need a fresh count, Blue Squad."

"copy that, Hawk. sorry, sir, this turbulence is givin us what for. i'm doin the best i can."

McKellar didn't respond.

"okay they're back in line, looping around, coming at the front-most bomber... zeroed in on that cockpit. our men are tight together. not a lot of room for error... lighting up that cockpit, first three zip by-- WHOA, pilot, TEN O'CLOCK!" the engine growled as the plane maneuvered. "number four spun out in the wash, came right at us. not sure if we'll see them again. okay, seeing if we can get a count... with the three that went by, and there's two more... man down! five left.. that's.. ten? shit, they just ripped through two more. they're going through us like crepe paper. circling around again, turning tight... okay, first birds headed back in nose to nose. made the pass-- holy hell, those heavy guns on the side just took out our first bird and the next two flew right through the debris, took them out, too. we're gettin low here."

"come on," David said under his breath. "just finish this one off first."

"east bomber is smoking, but still flying undeterred, looks like they got an engine fire? PILOT, BOGEYS! TWO O'CLOCK!"

bogeys?? David was terrified. he frantically scanned his map, where could those have come from?

two loud wooshes fried the airwaves. "oh hell yes! couple of F-100s outta nowhere!"

Mountain Home! David had written them off as too far away. but he hadn't calculated for Super Sabres, coming it at around 800 mph instead of 690 or so. maybe the rest of their squadron wouldn't be far behind.

"we got a little smoke... losing airspeed."

"stay with them," McKellar yelled.

two thuds were heard on the other end. "two more 84s gone! Sabre on fire, bowing out. F-100s are criss-crossing overhead trying to draw fire. another 86 down! i see... two 100s, three 84s... two 86s? 100s falling back behind them... five birds looping back around to the east bomber cockpit... both bombers sparkling... how much ammo do they have?" suddenly the speaker distorted with a loud B-BOOM. "whooo! go boys! make those Ruskies deaf."

"Blue 5 3, what's happening?" McKellar asked.

"sorry, sir, got caught up... never been that close to a sonic boom, much less two of them. F-100s zoomed up ahead. hard to hit something going the speed of sound... they're coming back around... 84s and 86s back in line... one down... two more smoking... damn, so close.. we're still losing airspeed, small smoking in our left wing. we'll be okay, but we can't keep up. i see chutes... looks like... three chutes, so i guess that's at least two more of ours down?" the sound of the Super Sabres screeching by again was unmistakable. "looks like the 100s got off a few. eastern bomber smoking pretty good, but still right in tandem with the other bomber."

"what's the status of the western bomber?" McKellar asked.

"hard to tell... we're still falling back.. seems like it's barely unscathed at this point, but we can't see the cockpit from here. F-100s have looped around, heading back upstream, burning afterburners... oh no.. one of them went nose up, trying to recover.. he's dancin all over the place.. he's spinning out..."

McKellar said shook his head. "they should have left those things grounded."

"sounds like we'd be toast without them," Boyd responded.

"our last three are comin at the bomber, guns a-blazin. Ruskies are givin it right back." the gunfire was faint, but three deep pops made their way above the wash of engine noise. "dammit! that's it for Ellsworth... last three fighters gone. one Super Sabre left in the fight.." another deep pop, and the radioman sighed. "man down.. one of those cannons got him from the side. he didn't have a chance. dammit!"

"all friendlies down, two bombers still incoming," Boyd announced.

"copy that," came the voice from SAC. "we could follow."

"where's the rest of the Mountain Home crew?" McKellar asked. he wasn't angry. that worried David.

David measured, looked at his watch, counted backwards, did the math in his head. "if they left at the same time... maybe five minutes, give or take?"

the radio shrieked to life again. "Hawk, this is Blue 5 3, come in."

McKellar lunged for the mic. "Blue 5 3, this is Hawk, we read you, over."

"eastern bomber is nosing down. the cockpit's ablaze."

"yes!" the celebration escaped Sollee's lips.

"whoa! that is one mega fireball. eastern bomber explodes over northern Wyoming. they'll be cleanin that up for a while."

"and the remaining bomber?"

"we still have a blip. they're maintaining course and airspeed. we're losing visual. wish we could have been more help."

"i pray you land safely," McKellar said, a genuine prayer in his voice.

"roger that, Colonel. Blue 5 3, over and out."

§

Partridge

Boyd squinted at the board. "who's next?"

"maybe Mountain Home," David said. "otherwise it's Wendover, near Casper." he traced his finger down the flight path, down from Casper, through Laramie, into Denver.

"oh shit," Roberts said, standing upright. "N.A.S. Denver. they're gonna be heading right into this thing."

everyone had forgotten. Boyd picked up the green telephone and set it in front of Walter. he started flipping through the directory.

David checked his map. "Lieutenant, find out when they left, please."

Walter nodded as he spun the rotary.

Boyd looked at Walter and Pepper. "we need ears and eyes with Mountain Home and Wendover."

"we've got frequencies for both," said the voice from SAC. "standby." Walter and Pepper waited, pencils in hand.

everyone else used the gap in fighting to breathe. those who were sitting stood. those who were standing sat. David just kept pacing behind his map. Howard was looking up at Gordy and

Leonard, still on the phones. he was working on something, David could see it in his brow.

Howard slowly stepped to Roberts. "this phone thing was pretty inconvenient."

"inconvenient?" Roberts said, stressing the understatement. he saw the look on Howard's face, too. "what you got cookin."

"you think it was on purpose? like, spies?"

"at Sears?"

"all they'd have to do is call in the ad."

Roberts stood up, and thought about it. "airman, i hope we last long enough to find out."

"N.A.S. Denver is still on the ground," Walter shouted.

"what?" McKellar shouted. David wasn't sure why he was even surprised at this point.

"they were waiting on a command from us, we never gave them one."

"order them in the air," Boyd said. "and give them Michaels' heading."

Walter scribbled a note, ripped it out, and lobbed it at Pepper.

"we need an ETA on N.A.S. Denver, Michaels."

"yessir."

David looked at his watch. his mother taught him how to tell time. with Grandnanny's clock on the mantle. big hand. little hand. she tested him on it. she reset the clock five different times, and David got it each time. she was so proud of him. she reached behind the clock and pulled out a model kit, five different planes. Mustang. P-39, P-40. RAF Typhoon and Spitfire. he found out later it had cost a whole dollar. he didn't have many toys, so they were all he played with, day and night. he'd stick one in his pocket. he got in trouble for sneaking one into church once. he loved those planes. David wondered if she'd got him a toy tow truck if he'd have become a mechanic instead. a *man's heart deviseth his way*, David thought, *but The Lord directeth his steps*. what verse was that? David walked over to his Bible, still on the floor, and walked it to the table. he flipped through the proverbs.

McKellar lifted the mic. "Mountain Home, Alpha 1 1. this is Hawk, come in, do you read us? over."

"copy that, Hawk. this is Alpha 1 1, we read you loud and clear, over."

"what's your twenty, over?"

"we're about seven minutes out. got the blip and changed heading. we had two blips, but only seeing one now. we were told there were three?"

"affirmative, Alpha 1 1, Blue Squad destroyed two contacts. final contact still on target."

suddenly David's bible was ripped out of his hands. Mo took the bible, still open and tossed it into the wastebasket.

"hey!" David chased him down.

"get your nose out of that fairy tale and pay attention!"

"Bonner!" Freeman yelled. Mo stopped, frozen. he didn't say a word, but his whole posture was a challenge. David went for the waste basket. "you too, Michaels. both of you man your posts." David looked at his Bible in the trash. then at Mo, who wouldn't look back.

"yes, sir." David snatched his grease pencil off the table and moved back behind the plexiglas. Mo moved toward the radio and stood, arms crossed, eyes staring past the floor. Captain Freeman slowly released his glare from Mo and returned his attention to McKellar at the radio mic. David glanced to Boyd, only to see him staring right at him. it made David's skin tingle and tighten.

"still waiting on that ETA for N.A.S. Denver, airman," Boyd said.

"yes, sir." David got to calculating. he tried three times in his head, but his anger at Mo kept creeping in and pushing the numbers out. he grabbed a pencil and pad to do his figuring. his hands were shaking. he scratched out a sketch, added numbers, did his math. then grabbed a red grease pencil and went to the board. "NAS Denver is about 20 minutes out. but looks like the rest of the Mountain Home squadron will intercept about 60 miles north of Casper, with Wendover not far behind."

McKellar nodded, hopeful. "they're gonna need the help."

"Michaels." Boyd had that same look on his face, still.

"sir?"

"12, not 14."

what was he talking about?

"the F-100s are gone, Michaels," McKellar said, irritated.

David had forgotten they were from Mountain Home. that's right. maybe Mo was right; maybe he should have been paying more attention. so that's twelve now. and twelve from Wendover. twenty-four fighters against the final bomber. what little hope David had left circled the drain as he stared at his own figures on the glass chart. the odds weren't great.

Howard moseyed over to the edge of the map wall. David eyed him until he appeared at the corner. "you okay?"

"i'm fine." David looked back through the glass at his bible in the trash.

"you can get it back when we make it through this."

"if," David said, correcting him.

"when," Howard stressed.

"my Grandpappy gave me that bible when i got baptized."

"you'll get it back, Michaels. let's just get through this first." David wanted to believe him. five minutes until everyone converged in the air near Casper. David would give anything to

132

spend those five minutes reading proverbs. everyone on the pit floor stood, waiting. phones still ringing in the tiers.

Tilday, Milton, and Froggy were still frantically making calls in the cab. at least no news was good news from them; if there were any more Soviet craft in the air, they'd have heard about it by now.

David looked around. "shouldn't Marston be back with the Colonel by now?"

"if you'd gotten to leave," Howard said, "would you come back?"

David wondered how far down Route 40 he'd be if he'd had those keys. "i hope he never comes back."

"i do."

"why? you think the Colonel can help in some way?"

"i don't know. but Marston has my truck."

David stared at Howard. Howard stared back, then winked. David chuckled. then laughed. his skin loosened and his heart rate slowed. he took a deep breath. he looked at his watch. the laugh faded. "four minutes, sir."

"Lieutenant Colonel Boyd," came the voice from SAC. "we have General Partridge on the party line."

"copy that, Colonel. hello, General."

"Boyd."

"two bombers are down, a final one still headed for Colorado Springs--"

"i've been briefed. i pray Wendover and the remaining fighters from Mountain Home are enough to bring this last bomber to the ground. but i need to make a few things very clear. these are all things you've probably thought of, but i'm making an official statement and official orders."

"roger that, sir."

"first, we need to be frank about the reality of the next hour. if the incoming fighters cannot intercept and neutralize the target, it is a sure certainty that the CONAD Command Center will be destroyed in total, and with it all of our communications and intelligence preparations from the last... well, the last ten years."

"yes, General, we've already put together a contingency communication plan--"

"yes, Boyd, i've been briefed on that as well. what i'm getting at is, we need a point of no return. if the bomber makes it through the squadrons from Wendover and Mountain Home, i order SAC to implement your contingency plan immediately for the sake of the national security of the United States."

the Command Center was a vacuum. every soul sucked away. hollow, uniformed shells remaining.

"copy that, General," Boyd said somberly. Boyd had already prepared everyone for it. but preparation was different than the real thing.

"second. we've not heard any word about nuclear explosions from the first two bombers, but we know they were protecting the final bomber, which is still in the air. if there's a nuclear weapon headed your way, it's on that third bomber. i know we would all like to avoid unnecessary collateral damage, but our primary concern is preserving the integrity of our communications hub at CONAD. it's likely whatever bomb they have is armed, coming in hot. simply blowing up the plane could cause it to explode in mid-air, sending fallout across the northern midwest. on the other hand, downing the plane could instigate an altitude-based trigger, causing it to explode just above ground, where it will do the most damage, especially if it's still inside a Tupolev 4 bomber. it would be like a nuclear grenade, sending flaming shrapnel hurtling for miles. an explosion of the magnitude we expect is enough to destroy most of Denver in seconds. we don't know how hard it will be to bring down that plane, or to destroy it in the air, or how long it will take, or what the casualties will be. so i can't give you — or the squadrons from Mountain Home and Wendover — specific orders based on weighing the various consequences. but what i can do is give this clear order: top priority is keeping that package from reaching CONAD, however you do it. we all want to avoid collateral damage, but we are facing the survival and protection of the U.S. military, who in turn protects every American man, woman, and child. and the sooner we neutralize this package, the better it will be for the city of Denver. and for CONAD and Colorado Springs."

"yes, sir."

"now, how long until Wendover reaches course?"

"Alpha 1 1, this is Hawk, do you read, over?"

"roger, Hawk, this is Alpha 1 1. minute and a half to target."

"where's Wendover?" Boyd asked, looking at David's chart.

"four more minutes for Wendover, sir."

"why weren't more squadrons sent our way, sir?" McKellar shouted.

"we sent what we thought was more than enough based on the intelligence at hand," the General replied. "CONAD's not the only place we're trying to protect. once the war begins, it's going to be mostly SAC communicating directly with Colonels in their respective theaters of operation anyway. having CONAD out of commission will hurt a lot. it will be a major setback to be sure, but that doesn't mean we stop trying to protect Washington, the East and West power grids, major nuclear power stations, our communications manufacturers--"

"so Oak Ridge and South Bend are more important than us?"

"they are still important and still need to be protected, even when CONAD Command no longer needs protecting."

"because why protect a crater," McKellar said. Boyd shot him a reprimanding look, but McKellar just glared at the black telephone.

the General took a deep breath. "i know tension is elevated, but we must rely on our training where we can. if this were a bombing run, and our radioman was taken out, we would continue with the mission at hand, and someone else would get on the radio as they could. we have to do the same. at this point, tell me what other option we have."

the pit floor was silent.

"then stop throwing this circumstance back at me like i'm the one that caused it, like i don't sympathize with what is about to happen there, and like i'm not giving you direct orders which you are to follow." the General's voice got more and more forceful with each clause, making David's blood colder and colder.

"yes, sir." Major McKellar said, his tone changed. his whole posture was different. he was no longer the loudest voice in the room. he pushed Boyd around, but couldn't do that with General Partridge.

"now how long until Mountain Home and Wendover reach the package?"

"Mountain Home should be acquiring visual any second, sir," said Boyd. he startled, surprised to see Marston standing next to him. he spun around. "Colonel..."

everyone turned to see the Colonel standing in the dark doorway of the tunnel. David wondered if they should salute, but it seemed as if the time for that was over. the Colonel stood there quietly.

"welcome back, sir." Boyd said, standing taller.

the Colonel walked slowly to the makeshift war room they'd assembled on the pit floor. he walked to the mapboards, looked around at the tapestry, at David's markings, at David's Santa Claus, the bottom half smeared away revealing the enemy trajectory. he looked up across the tiers, into the cab.

"Colonel," said Partridge. "we've been wondering where you were."

"i'm here," the Colonel said, looking around. "we should have built this place underground."

"we'll... take that under advisement," said Partridge.

Boyd walked to him. "sir, how much of that did you hear?" Boyd asked him quietly. David could barely hear him through the glass.

"enough that part of me wishes i'd stayed home."

David understood; better to do die in an ignorant instant than spend your last few minutes alive at work, dreading your inevitable death.

"but i belong here with my men. even if..." his eyes stayed locked on the phones.

"... there's nothing we can do," Boyd finished.

"is there nothing we can do?" the Colonel asked?

"Hawk, this is Alpha 1 1... we have visual. thirty seconds to firing range."

"copy that, Alpha 1 1." McKellar lowered the mic. "sirs, respectfully, we're not out of this yet."

a phone in the tiers rang. it was the first ring David had heard in a few minutes. the calls had been dying down, and with all that was going on, he'd not even noticed. Gordy answered it. Leonard sat, watching the activity on the floor.

"can we just unplug those now?" Roberts asked Boyd

"no," the Colonel said. "keep Cesana and Gordy on the phones as long as calls keep coming in."

"sir, you still want to keep our men answering these ridiculous Santa calls?"

"my daughter is one of those kids," the Colonel snapped. Roberts sobered instantly and stood straight before his superior. "she's been calling all night trying to get through. and i want her to think everything is going to be okay. i don't want her to think there's no one watching, no one who cares if she's good or bad, if she sleeps, if she lives. i want her to know someone is watching out for her. and i want them to stay on those phone until she gets through. until they all get through."

Roberts' shoulders slowly sank. David understood. this wasn't just geopolitics or mass war. it was about the freedom of every family — every person — to survive. the Colonel's family. David's family. David. and, surviving, free to be happy. among life, liberty, and the pursuit of happiness, David had always been convinced that life came first. but he was starting to think... maybe they weren't three separate things.

"i apologize, sir." Roberts voice was sincere, its usual edge vanished.

the Colonel straightened his uniform jacket. "there's nothing for them to do down here anyway. any problems with that, General, sir?"

"no, Colonel. i trust you with your men."

"Hawk come in, this is Alpha 1 1, over."

McKellar pressed the mic button. "we read you, Alpha 1 1."

Boyd stepped toward the radio. "here we go..."

§

hang your stockings and say your prayers

"okay, Hawk, Alpha Squad on the approach. contact incoming. eleven birds a-firin. damn, that's a thing a beauty."

"86 the commentary, 1 1."

"roger that, Hawk. my apologies. Soviet Tu-4 lit up like a parade float, gunfire from all over the place." a few dinks cut into the engine noise. "holy hell, how are they hitting us way out here. moving farther out of range. standby."

"what's happening with the bomber, Alpha 1 1," asked McKellar, frustrated.

"i lost visual... give us a second, Hawk. we gotta circle back around to the front." the engine noise leveled out. "creeping forward... okay, hard to see too clearly, but we still got a lot of planes in the air. i do see a few chutes, though. and i see a little smoke from one wing of the bomber. our boys coming back around..."

"get us a count, Alpha 1 1."

"roger that. we got... nine left, besides us... looks like they're pulling together into combat box..."

"didn't we tell them trail formation, right at the cockpit?" McKellar said to Boyd.

Boyd shrugged. "SAC, what instructions have you given the Mountain Home team?"

"standard combat box. lead element goes for the cockpit, high and low elements go for the jet engines on the wings. our team here believes this will be the most effective."

McKellar tossed a look at Boyd. David saw it, and so did the Colonel.

"SAC makes the strategic calls here, Major," the Colonel said.

"yes, sir," McKellar said through a poker face. "i guess that's what the S is for." Boyd laid a hand on his shoulder, but said not a word.

"box comin in. cockpit sparkling with ricochet.. glass! looks like we broke somethin... more glass.. and the box has passed... circling around for another go at it... looks like we lost a fighter out of the lead element, it's diving... i lost visual on it." the engines roared. "standby, Hawk." and the radio cut out. it was back in seconds. "we've been ordered to join the box, Hawk. circling around to the low element on the far side."

"watch those cannons on the side, Alpha 1 1."

"copy that, Hawk. i'll relay to the lead element. standby." the radio cut out, and came back. "okay, we're going in." the engine revved and the patter of pops grew louder as they passed the wing. several booms were heard.

"we lost a few on that one. you weren't kiddin about those heavy guns, Hawk. i think we did some damage on the wings, but hard to tell. they're pretty layered up. hey, any idea what this thing is under the wing?"

McKellar and Boyd looked at each other. they looked at Freeman and Roberts. "describe it," McKellar said.

"well, it kinda looked like a MiG, but smaller."

McKellar set the mic down. "is it like an escape plane or something?"

"no," Roberts said. "it's a rocket."

"like a V2?" Howard asked.

"may be," Boyd said. "except not ground to air."

"air to air?" Freeman asked.

Boyd sighed. "my bet is air to ground."

"for us," Roberts said.

"they're that confident in their aim to use a missile?" Freeman asked.

"the Nazis had guided missiles during the war," Boyd said. "Russia is building on everything they had."

"well why the hell don't we have any?" McKellar said.

"we're developing them," Boyd said.

McKellar just shook his head.

"you think they'd hang their nuclear weapon off a wing?" Roberts asked.

"no," said Boyd. "but with all this trouble, i think they'd have a backup."

McKellar pounded the mic. "get that MiG, Alpha 1 1."

"copy that, Hawk." the engines revved again, the pops of gunfire were heard again, followed by a large boom. "cockpit exploded! i think we blew up one of their rockets right in their commie faces!" a loud whoosh screeched through. "wooo! barely evaded a collision with that MiG... the MiG is loose, i repeat, the MiG is loose... circling around for it." another large boom. "bomber is a fireball... took a few of ours with it."

"nuclear explosion?" McKellar asked.

"if it were a nuke, i think they'd be dead, too," Roberts said.

"negative, Hawk. just a big bottlerocket, flaming pieces floating to the ground."

the engines whined and screamed, and then leveled out, slowly revving up to full tilt. "we got four birds left, all in pursuit of this MiG. i can't see it, it's dead ahead of us, though. we're unloading everything we got at it." the barrage of pops confirmed it. "hang on, i see it. it's weavin all over the damn place."

"stay after it, Alpha 1 1."

"Hawk, we're all at top speed chasin this thing, and the blip is getting farther away."

"this thing is outpacing an F-86?" Freeman said.

"it's not a MiG, it's a rocket," Roberts said. "no cockpit. no munitions. no landing gear. just a jet engine and fuel. and a warhead."

"it must be a Komet," the Colonel said.

"comet?" Walter said.

"yes, with a K. Soviet Kometa. i've heard them rumored, but we weren't sure they really existed."

"well, it does," Boyd said. "and it's on its way. get Wendover on the radio."

Pepper began dialing in the radio.

"Colonel," said Partridge over the speaker, "i'm invoking my orders."

"we still have the group from Wendover, dammit!" McKellar yelled at the General.

"and i pray they are able to stop this thing. but we have the rest of this war to fight."

"so what does this mean, sir" the Colonel asked.

"you can stay on the party line if you like," Partridge replied. McKellar shook his head, disgusted. "but, i don't see the point in it now. SAC has initiated contact with the critical towers using your contingency plan — quite an impressive thing to put together in such a short time. and we'll leave you Wendover. any other non-fighter, non-bomber in your range is in your hands as well. command at will."

"that's very generous, General," the Colonel huffed.

"we don't like it either, Colonel," the General retorted. "but we have a war to fight. Godspeed." and the SAC line went dead.

"well. that's that," Roberts said.

the Colonel picked up the black handset and slammed it onto its base.

"frankly, i'll be happy not to have the interruption," said McKellar, red.

Pepper nodded at McKellar.

"come in Omega 1 1, this is Hawk, over."

"Hawk, this is Omega 1 1, we read you load and clear."

"be advised: target course is the same, but speed has increased to beyond 650 miles per hour."

David realized he'd have to adjust his map, all of his times, all the suggested headings for everything incoming.

"we're two minutes from original course, Hawk, please advise."

David frantically started calculating, then realized he didn't have an airspeed for this rocket. he turned to the Colonel. "how fast is this thing going?"

"no idea."

"if it's just outrunning our 86s," Roberts said, "then it's gotta be right at 700 mph."

David quickly made grease marks from where Wendover was to where they needed to go, almost a full 90 degrees off of where there headed now. when McKellar saw it, his eyes got big.

"Omega 1 1, alter Omega Team course to 120°, full speed."

"roger that! standby!" and the transmission went quiet as the radioman relayed the orders to the rest of his wing. when the line went live again, the engine noise was remarkable. "what are we chasing, Hawk?"

"we think it's a Komet," McKellar yelled, hoping the radioman could hear him over the jet noise.

"a comet?" asked the radioman.

"affirmative," affirmed McKellar, "and i spell, King Oboe Mike Easy Tare. Soviet ballistic projectile."

"copy that, Hawk. how many, over?"

"just one."

just, David thought.

the engines blasted full speed, loudly. Pepper turned the volume down some, but the white noise crawled across David's skin and through his hair.

"ah we see it on radar, Hawk. this thing is screaming."

"roger, Omega 1 1. just get it. whatever it takes."

"is this a manned craft? it's pitching and yawing every which way."

"negative."

"never seen anything like this. all twelve of us are coming at it. in firing range shortly. twenty seconds."

"sir, i need an exact airspeed."

"Omega 1 1, can you get us an exact airspeed for the Komet, over."

"coming up on it. letting loose." gunfire peppered the transmission. "it's gone by, but we're close on it. still in range."

"i need a speed, airman," McKellar shouted.

"we're at 660 miles per hour. it's outpacing us... gotta be close to 700."

"i need it exact, airman."

"okay.. standby... ...blip one is 600 yards out... blip two... 1,113 yards away. sweep time is three and a half seconds..."

David was scratching figures and multiplying, using his slide ruler, solving equations. "690 miles an hour," he exclaimed and ran to the mapboards, altering his markings.

"if we've hit it, you'd never know it," said the man in the air. "not sure if we'll be out of ammo or out of range first. it's dashing and dancing all over the place."

the din of gunfire splashed for a few more seconds, then ebbed away.

"contact has escaped unscathed. repeat, contact is still in play."

"copy that, Omega 1 1. you belong to SAC now. Godspeed. over and out."

and before a response could come in, Pepper was whipping dials around. he landed on his frequency, and nodded to Major McKellar.

"Naval Air Station Denver, this is Hawk, come in."

the radio popped in with a loud whoosh. "we read you, Hawk. this is NAS Den 1 1. expect to acquire target in a few minutes."

"copy that. it's coming right at you. best if half your squadron goes right at it, the other half goes halfway out and turns back to come alongside."

"wilco, Hawk, standby while i relay." and the air was silent.

"i'm not gonna wait on sailors," McKellar said, an eyeroll in his voice. "what comes after this?"

"that's it," Freeman said, looking at the board. "that was our last line of defense."

"hey, what about Francis E. Warren?" Marston asked, pointing to the base on one of David's charts, still hanging on the mapboards.

"Warren doesn't even have a runway," Roberts said. "all they have is choppers."

"that's *something*," Howard said.

"if we couldn't catch it with fighter jets, we're not going to catch it with a couple of whirlybirds," McKellar said.

"maybe they'll get off a lucky shot," Boyd said.

"against a missile going seven hundred miles an hour? they don't have a prayer."

"well, then maybe we should give them one."

and the room fell silent.

David looked at his fellow airmen. most just stood there, stunned. McKellar's eyes drifted across his lap. Sollee bowed his head. Mo stared right at David. he was dead already. David stared back, stared into his dead eyes.

please, God, David prayed. that was it. just, *please, God*.

not even the phones were ringing. Gordy sat in the tiers, listening. Leonard got up and walked to the floor.

Tilday, Milton, and Froggy exited the cab and walked slowly down the stairs, pallbearers of an unseen coffin.

"Warren has four choppers they can put in the air," Walter said, breaking the silence. "they're fully arming them now, and will be sending them up within the next two minutes."

"got it," said Boyd. "thank you, Lieutenant." Boyd looked at the cab crew as they joined them on the floor.

"SAC gave us the boot," said Major Tilday. Boyd nodded.

"what's happening now?" Captain Milton asked.

"our lives are in the hands of a handful of chopper pilots and some sailor reserves," the Colonel said.

none of them reacted. Leonard hovered over their shoulders. Gordy came down and sat on the floor beside Mo.

"Hawk, this is NAS Den 1 1, come in, over."

"we're here, NAS Den 1 1, over."

"six of us are breaking off and turning back, hoping to come up along side it. they're gonna go two by two. NAS Den 3 1 shares our frequency and will be your eyes if it gets that far."

"fantastic. copy that, NAS Den 1 1."

"we're approaching in combat box with lead and high elements. we're going to just crossfire this thing."

"whatever it takes, sailor."

"aye, aye, Hawk. standby. we've got the contact on radar, approaching. spreading out the vee so we can get a good crossfire pattern on it. in firing range in... 5... 4... 3... 2... aaand.. let 'em rip!" the gunfire could be heard from the Naval planes. David couldn't help but think about these men a little differently. not because they were Navy, but because they were Reserves. so many Reserves made the commitment knowing they may be called up one day, but he doubted they were prepared for specialized combat like this. not prepared in their training, and not prepared in their hearts. until they were commanded into the air, they probably sat twiddling their thumbs, wishing they were home for Christmas. kind of like David felt, hours ago, when things were boring. *dear God*, David prayed, *please make things boring again.*

"damn! that was fast. it got by us. we got off a few shots on it, i could see the sparks. must have glanced off. guess it's armored up pretty good. plus, it's whipping around all over. we did our best to shower it, but... sorry, fellas. handing you off to NAS Den 3 1, Hawk. over and out."

"copy that, NAS Den 1 1." McKellar set the mic down and scratched his forehead. "that was a waste."

"the other six will have more time," Boyd said. "flying with it instead of against it."

"Hawk, this is NAS Den 3 1, over."

"we read you, NAS Den 3 1. it's headed your way."

"roger that, Hawk. we're in a wide inverted vee with parallel pairs. hoping to converge on it without blowing our squad mates' assess off."

"sounds like as good a plan as any, sailor," McKellar said.

"yes sir. like a giant zipper!" David thought the sailor's voice sounded even younger than Marston or Burke.

"what if bullets aren't enough?" Roberts asked.

"what difference does it make if that's all we have?" McKellar asked.

"it's not all we have," Roberts said.

"you think these Navy Reserve jets have missiles?" Freeman said.

"i think these Navy Reserve jets," Roberts replied, "*are* missiles."

Boyd closed his eyes. McKellar nodded somberly. the Colonel stepped over to the radio. McKellar looked up. the Colonel sighed, then nodded.

"here it comes! in our six... three, one o'clock, FIRE!" light gunfire dotted the air. "jeez louise what's this thing made of??" the gunfire stopped. "we might have hit it two or three times, and from the looks of it, it didn't make a bit of difference--"

"sailor, this is Hawk with a direct order. instruct the two remaining pairs to converge on the incoming missile."

"yes, sir, that's the plan, sir."

"no, sailor. physically converge on it. put your aircraft in its path."

the radio was silent.

"NAS Den 3 1, do you copy?"

"uh.. yes.. Hawk... we copy, standby."

and the radio was silent again.

"we have no other choice," the Colonel said to McKellar. McKellar stared at the radio mic.

"roger, Hawk. relayed the orders."

"roger, 3 1."

"okay watching my blips.. the pair ahead of us are converging.. contact is approaching. i got three blips together. i have visual on an explosion up ahead."

everyone on the pit floor leaned forward. David could see his breath on the glass.

"NAS Den 3 1, is the target down?"

every hesitation was gut-wrenching.

"we still have a blip headed your way."

"is it the rocket or one of yours."

"i see... four chutes. the package is still alive."

"holy hell," the Colonel said, "they crashed into each other.

"dammit," cursed Roberts.

"get your forward pair out of parallel so that doesn't happen again."

"copy that, standby while i relay."

Roberts paced. it was the first real anxiety David had seen from him. he must feel responsible for those lives. surely he knows it's not his fault.

"these two planes might be our last hope," the Colonel said.

"okay, Hawk, lead pair converging, but that blip is headed in fast.. it's about to escape our radar range."

"stay on it," said McKellar.

"we're at top speed, sir. forward pair just entered our radar. converging. staggered. i.. don't think they're going to make it... coming up on the first plane... he didn't make it.. got by him."

groans and sighs crawled across the pit floor.

"last plane... getting close... i see two blips.. coming together... at the edge of our radar... lost it... don't see an explosion... standby..."

"no explosion means no explosion," Boyd said, grave.

"come in, Hawk, that's a big negative. he met it in the sky, but it pitched up just before impact, it tapped his wing, but is still headed your way."

"roger, NAS Den 3 1. Godspeed, over and out."

"over and out."

and the radio was silent again.

§

o little town

everyone sulked.

David winced his eyes shut, holding back tears. he prayed in his heart. he emptied everything, and he sank. it was the greatest fear and sadness he'd ever met. he crawled under the devastating froth, and underneath, there was an eddy of joy, because God was there. he struggled to chase, but it slipped further away. he let go of his fear, his sadness. the vortex swelled. he gave up the last he had, his breath, his life. David was dead. the whirlpool devoured him and thrust him through, a peel of sunlight burned his face, threatened to pierce his eyelids as he rose...

he took a breath and opened his eyes.

everyone sulked.

except David.

"guys, we're already dead." David wasn't sad. or scared. he was bold. "there's nothing else to be afraid of. let's try anything. anything at all. no matter how crazy--"

"David," Boyd said, with his fatherly tone.

"we gotta at least try, sir. it's just ideas. if we come up with a good one, you can make it happen. and if we don't..."

"we die trying," Roberts finished.

Boyd stood. "ideas. go."

no one moved. no one spoke.

"listen. we have about twenty-two minutes until the Soviet package arrives. SAC has moved on to the coasts."

"they abandoned us," Mo said.

"they sent us four squadrons plus."

"that wasn't enough," Mo objected. the Colonel stared at him. "sir."

Boyd wasn't having it. "nowhere else in the world will it be 20 to 1 up against a Soviet bomber. they sent us more than anyone thought reasonable. and no. it wasn't enough." he walked over to David's chart of Colorado and thrust a finger onto the red line. "twenty-two minutes until this gets here. we're our last defense. if anything is to be done about our survival, it's totally on us. if anything..." Boyd pointed toward the tiers, swallowed, and continued, "is to be done about the survival of the children of our little town... it's on *us*. so. any suggestions?"

Leonard was always first. "we shoot it."

"we've tried that," Roberts said. "shells aren't doing much to it, and it's moving too fast anyway."

"he asked for ideas, Major. i'm giving ideas."

"thank you, Airman, and i'm giving you the reason it won't work. next idea."

"what about a net?" Gordy asked.

"a twenty-thousand-foot-tall net?"

"...between ...two planes?"

"seriously?"

"... behind one plane?"

"between two copters!" Sollee said. "from Warren. we have that. we can make that happen. they have all kinds of netting and webbing from training--"

"assuming the copters can fly it up and keep it up, two big *ifs*," Roberts said, "how big a target is that? maybe thirty foot square? besides, this thing is going nearly 700 miles an hour. it'd shred right through it. it might not even slow down."

"what if we tow it away, somehow, like a glider," Burke offered.

"how?"

"with... a... cable?"

"but how, Burke. how are you gonna get the cable on it?"

Burke thought.

Froggy jumped in. "hey, didn't we snatch gliders during the war?"

"yeah!" Walter said, getting up. "the plane would come in low with a tow cable, snatch the glider and yank it out of there."

"yes," said the Colonel. "but the glider had a tow cable suspended like a volleyball net for the very purpose of being caught by the tow hook of the plane. there's no way to grab ahold of this thing."

"what about a magnet," Captain Freeman asked. "on a tow cable?"

McKellar frowned. "i can't think of a single craft equipped with--"

"yeah, yeah, but if we had one somehow. somewhere between here and Laramie, someone's got a magnet."

"it doesn't matter," Roberts said. "your whole glider premise starts with a stationary target."

"yeah but pilots can get that close to a moving target," Walter continued. "that guy that flew his crop-duster for like 45 days straight--"

"45 days? bull,shit." Gordy said.

"i swear! anyone else know what i'm talking about?"

"he's right, i remember that," McKellar said. "some kind of publicity stunt. it was a biplane, i think. he'd float over a Ford pickup on this blocked off straightaway going like a hundred miles an hour. they'd refuel from a big tank in the bed of the truck." Gordy was stunned. it sounded vaguely familiar to David, maybe some story Howard told him. some others clearly knew about it and a few others clearly thought it was made up.

"guys, this thing is going seven hundred miles an hour, not a hundred," Roberts said.

"refueling!" Marston said. "we get a refueling tanker--"

"how many more times am i gonna have to say it, SEVEN HUNDRED MILES AN HOUR. fighters don't refuel going top speed. and refueling tankers barely go half that at top speed."

"what about," Leonard demonstrated with his hands, "a bomber with its bomb doors open lowers down on top of it as it passes by? then we just shut the doors around it and fly it away?" he was really proud of this idea.

Roberts snorted a pathetic chuckle, shaking his head harder, and counted his points on his fingers. "you're not gonna get a bomber to go seven hundred miles an hour, definitely not with the doors open, as soon as you get inside the airspace of this bomb — which is weaving all over the damn place — the thrust is going to shoot it through the cockpit, tearing our fictional turbo-speed bomber apart, likely exploding directly over Denver in the process."

Leonard was less proud of his idea. he plopped down on the floor next to Gordy. "we shoulda stayed by the phones."

"what about an Atlas rocket?" Gordy asked.

Sollee lit up. "yeah! or the... Titan? is that the new one?"

"we can't hit it with thousands of five cent rounds from yards away, so you want to try to hit it with a single multi-million dollar rocket from the ground?" said Major McKellar.

"doesn't matter," Boyd said. "closest operable rocket is in San Diego."

"i thought they were building a place south of Denver?" Howard said.

"they are. they break ground in February," Boyd said.

"dammit," Howard said, expressing everyone's frustration.

"what about a Nike?" Captain Milton offered.

"nearest one is in New Mexico," Roberts said.

"what if we put bazookas on a chopper?" David said.

everyone looked at each other.

then everyone looked at Roberts. when he realized it, he sat up. "well. it's the least terrible idea we have."

"i'll take it," Boyd said. "McKellar--"

"on it." McKellar was already huddled with Marston looking up the number for the Warren base.

"i said shoot it," Leonard said. "that's the first thing i said."

"can it, Lenny."

"get bent, Howard."

Roberts tossed them an exasperated glare. "guys."

"i need to talk to one of your choppers on the VHF." McKellar scribbled a note, green receiver tucked under his ear. Pepper watched him write. "copy that." and he slammed the phone down, ripped out the note and handed to Pepper. Pepper was already dialing it in. McKellar grabbed the mic. "Warren 1 1, this Hawk, do you read, over."

"this is Warren 1 1... is this CONAD Command? over."

McKellar huffed. "yes, dammit. listen we need your choppers to have every rocket launcher you can get on board."

"we're already in the air, sir."

"then land, get every rocket launcher at Francis E. Warren Air Force Base, and get back in the air."

there was a long silence.

"uh, sir... we're ten minutes from base.. i don't think we can go back and make it back in time. "

David panicked, grabbed his ruler, and ran to his board. he measured. that's what he was afraid of. "sirs, they can't make it, even at top speed."

"okay forget it, Warren," McKellar sighed. "full speed ahead. use what you have."

"uh, no, Major," David clarified. "they can't make it. they're still seven minutes out at least. this thing will be way past them by then."

McKellar leaned back in his chair. Boyd stepped up to the mapboard to look. David sat on the edge of the table.

"call them off," Boyd said.

McKellar leaned up to the mic. "stand down, Warren."

"come again, sir?"

"stand down. go home. over and out."

§

adeste fideles

David could hear the slow crinkle of cellophane from the rotating light of the aluminum tree. every airman was silent; not present, minds awol. they were all together in the pit, but each of them was alone with naked fear.

Mo got up and walked to his phonograph. he carefully set the arm of the turntable onto the spinning 45. the dust and scratches popped through the air like snowflakes blanketing a window. an old recording of a celeste began to play Silent Night through the tinny built-in speaker. everyone turned to look at Mo. everyone but David.

Mo walked toward the utility room, reached into the wastebasket, and retrieved David's Bible. he walked to where David sat, laid it down on the table, and pushed it toward him. David looked at him; his eyes were red and damp. Mo turned away and slid down into a corner, ankles crossed, elbows on his knees, eyes locked on David.

David opened the Bible and flipped through its gold-leafed pages until he found his ribbon. he lifted the Bible into his hands and cleared his throat.

"...and it came to pass... in those days, that there went out a decree from Caesar Augustus, that all the world should be taxed, and this taxing was first made when Cyrenius was governor of Syria..."

Gordy and Leonard watched David read.

"and all went to be taxed, every one into his own city. and Joseph also went up from Galilee, out of the city of Nazareth, into Judea, unto the city of David, which is called Bethlehem, because he was of the house and lineage of David..."

David looked up, to see if there would be any protest. the Colonel stood at ease, his hands clasped behind him. Boyd was sitting on the tier steps, listening.

"...to be taxed with Mary his espoused wife, being great with child."

one by one, every airman, every officer came closer to the table. some stood. some sat on the floor. Walter knelt. the celeste played quietly over the intercom. it was sacred.

"...and so it was, that, while they were there, the days were accomplished that she should be delivered. and she brought forth her firstborn son, and wrapped him in swaddling clothes, and laid him in a manger, because there was no room for them in the inn."

Mo closed his eyes as a tear finally escaped, and he rest his forehead on his arms.

"and there were in the same country shepherds abiding in the field, keeping watch over their flock by night. and, lo, the angel of the Lord came upon them, and the glory of the Lord shone round about them: and they were sore afraid."

David took a breath.

"and the angel said unto them, 'fear not! for, behold, I bring you good tidings of great joy, which shall be to all people. for unto you is born this day in the city of David a Savior, which is Christ *the Lord. and this shall be a sign unto you: ye shall find the babe wrapped in swaddling clothes, lying in a manger.'*

"and suddenly there was with the angel a multitude of the heavenly host praising God, and saying, 'Glory to God in the highest, and on earth..."

he stopped...

"... peace... good will toward men.' "

the gentle hymn concluded, echoing throughout this new cathedral. the pops and crackles increased until the arm lifted itself from the turntable and returned to rest. the church was silent.

Gordy sobbed quietly. the Colonel walked over to Gordy, sat beside him, and placed a hand on his shoulder.

Boyd stood. "thank you, David. men, can we... think about beautiful things for a few minutes?"

no one objected.

"God on earth."

"so humble."

"little baby."

"the love of a mother."

"peace is ... would be beautiful."

"King of the Universe came first to some shepherds."

"that would have been pretty neat," Gordy said.

"what's that?" said Howard.

"to see all those angels appear like that. you're just out in a field minding your own business. it's just a night like any other night. and then this angel appears out of nowhere, and then... hundreds of 'em."

"thousands," Leonard said.

a few men nodded their heads, trying to imagine.

"we could use a few thousand angels right about now," Walter said.

"a blinding light in the middle of the night." as soon as David said it, he realized what a blinding light tonight would mean.

"you think so?" Howard said. "i imagined them kinda like super bright stars shimmering in the sky."

Gordy shot up. "SHIMMER," he yelled. Leonard looked frightened; Gordy's face was all puffy and wet from weeping. he looked around, waiting for a response.

"what are you talking about, Gordy?" Walter asked.

"Shimmer! the... the.. D-Day thing."

"i'm lost," Howard said.

"Glimmer," said Boyd. "Operation Glimmer."

"right, okay, so... what does that have to do with anything?" Roberts asked.

"what's Operation Glimmer?" David asked.

Boyd straightened. "Operation Glimmer was a deception operation on D-Day. British bombers dropped aluminum chaff--"

" 'angel grass'!" Gordy interjected.

"--to float in the sky off the coast of Pas-de-Calais," Boyd continued, "way north of Normandy. Royal Navy ships underneath had radar bouncing balloons and sent out false radio signals mimicking RAF fleet chatter. to German radar, it'd look *and* sound like hundreds of planes were approaching for an air attack. the idea was to fool them into watching the air at Pas-de-Calais while we prepared to land ashore at Normandy."

"yeah, that's it!" Gordy was excited.

Mo got up. "so what is it Gordy, you want to try to fool the bomb into thinking we're actually in Salt Lake City?"

"yeah," Roberts interrupted. "what's the point of subterfuge at this point--"

Gordy was shaking his head. "no... angels! in the air! can't we dump chaff to explode the bomb way up in the air or something?"

Mo rolled his eyes. "good grief, Gordy, a blast that high could kill the power to half the country. we'd be putting SAC out of commission. and the fallout would blow halfway to Chicago--"

Boyd put a hand out to settle him. "blowing up a nuclear bomb in the air over Denver might not be a great idea..." Gordy's face dropped. "...but, if we could drop the chaff like a net. then capture it somehow. Michaels, how much time do we have?"

David, surprised, bolted up, back into action. he grabbed a couple of pages of notes and scratched out some figures. "about thirteen minutes."

"we need an exact time for a countdown. and a confirmed bearing and airspeed from the tower in Denver."

Burke hopped up, "i'm on it," and grabbed the green phone. Marston whipped through the tower directory.

"how do you capture it with aluminum chaff?" Walter asked.

Major Roberts spoke up. "you can't. it'd just get sucked into the intake. the aluminum could short out the electronics, metal ripping through the guts could burst the radioactive components--"

"what about water? like from a firefighting airtanker?" Gordy asked.

"that could electrocute it, cause it to detonate--"

"what about a powder flame retardant, like a sodium bicarbonate compound," Boyd said.

"baking soda." Roberts said, dubious.

"it will choke the missile's jet engine and cause a flameout, kill the engine. it'd just be a glider at that point. maybe that would slow it down enough that we can capture it some other way, tow it off to a safe place."

Leonard sat up. "wait... capture... so are all those other options back on the table?"

Roberts put a hand on Leonard's chest. "guys, stop, where are we going to get a British bomber full of baking soda in the next twelve minutes?"

Howard raised his hand. "how about a TBM Avenger full of shit?" everyone's head snapped to look.

"the tire fires," David said. it was brilliant. would it work?

Burke and Marston were on the green phone, scribbling notes. Howard shot up and bounded up the tiers.

"what are you doing?" Boyd asked.

"i'm calling Larry Todd Salvage Yard," he yelled over his shoulder.

"are you kidding me?" Mo shouted. "we have twelve minutes. it's 10 o'clock, Christmas Eve. his whole family's probably asleep."

"yeah, them and the rest of the Springs," Boyd said, heading up the stairs. "and they're never going to wake up if we don't try this."

Howard ran up the stairs and made for the red phone, still sitting outside the cab door. David held his hand out to Mo and lifted him from the ground. they followed most of the rest of the crew, filling the stairwell and spilling into the tiers.

Roberts pushed his way to the front. "wait a minute, what is the plan here?"

"drop a curtain of manure," Howard said, bent over, dialing. "the jet engine chokes on it, slows down. and we snatch it."

"with what?" Roberts asked.

Howard stood up. "it's ringing. hey it's Howard Alspach, can i please speak to Larry? it's an emergency. thank you."

"someone said magnet earlier," David said. "he's got to have some kind of magnet at a junkyard."

Howard covered the mouthpiece. "hey, we're gonna need precise instructions."

David scratched some figures on a nearby memo. Boyd and Roberts came over to look at David's notes.

"hang on," Roberts said. "you're going to have to get him as far north as you can to give this thing time to slow down. they're going to have to gain on it. they're in an Avenger, those things are slow. and they're going to have to get it before it drops to a certain altitude."

"right. the Komet might have an altitude-based trigger," Boyd said, grabbing Howard's arm. he opened the cab door and pulled him through, the long, red coil of phone cord slapping against the doorframe. Boyd reached down to the command console and flipped the speaker switch.

"this will get them headed in the right direction," David said, stepping into the cab. "we can give them specifics once they're in the air." he set it on the console in front of Howard.

"yhello?" came the folksy voice over the cab speaker.

"Larry! this is Howard."

"hey son, you said there was an emergency?"

"yessir, i'm at work--"

"at BJ's? y'all got a grease fire or somethin?"

"no, sir.. my new work."

"the secret Air Force thing?"

"yes. so you understand the nature of the emergency."

"...okay."

"we need a planeload of manure dropped like a curtain in front of an incoming rocket. then we need that rocket snatched in mid-air, maybe with a magnet..."

wow, it sounded really crazy to David, the way Howard just said it.

"do what now?"

Boyd stepped in and took the handset from Howard. "Larry, this is Lieutenant Colonel James Boyd. we have a rocket — basically tiny jet plane — headed to Colorado Springs from the north. the only way we can stop it is to slow it down. now, i've heard you're a master shitslinger."

"well.. my wife says so."

Boyd chuckled. "well, we need a wall of manure, dirt, whatever you've got. the debris will get sucked into the jet engine, hopefully cause it to fail. the rocket will then be a glider, going slower and slower. and we hope you're able to gain on it before it stalls out and capture it somehow and tow it away. if you had some kind of magnet, maybe on a long cable--"

"what's this thing weigh?"

"we're not sure. probably about six thousand pounds."

"hoo wee!"

"but it's airborne. your Avenger will be plenty to tow it."

"and where'm i towin it to?"

"we'll figure that out once we have it. is your bomber bay loaded?"

"yeah, it's fresh, too."

"and do you have a magnet and tow cable to catch the rocket?"

"well.. i got an industrial wench and some high-strength cable and... yeah i got a portable electromagnet. use it for pullin engines out of semis. when we doin this thing?"

"right now."

"now?"

"*right* now. you've got to get in the air as soon as possible."

"well i can't do this by myself. i'm going to need.. i need to get Kenny."

Howard's face fell.

"is this Kenny nearby?" Boyd asked.

"yessir, he's my grandson. he's the only one in the house who knows how to operate the wench and the electromagnet." Larry hesitated. "this little fishin trip... what are the chances we're comin back from this."

"that you even think to ask that question ought to give you an idea of the risks."

the other end of the phone was silent.

"Larry, we don't have time to waste. now, you're not one of my airmen, so i can't give you an order. but i can call on you as a brother, as an American."

"and if we don't do this...?"

"major destruction."

"the Springs?"

"... the entire U.S."

David could hear Larry's fidgeting. the whole cab stared at the speaker, as if Larry and Kenny might suddenly pop out of it to save the day.

"well hell. i guess it's damned if we do, damned if we don't, ain't it. Kenny! Kenny, get up, we gotta put out a fire!"

McKellar pushed forward. "Larry, you got a radio on that thing?"

"i got the original ART-13 so we can talk to whoever's on the ground."

"not long range enough for us," McKellar said. "what else do you have?"

"i got an ARC-5 in the den."

"in the den?"

"i jiggered it into a Ham."

"we can get on the ham band with the shortwave," Mo said from the doorway, excited. David smiled at him.

"take the ARC-5 with you, Larry." McKellar whispered to Pepper. "get me a frequency."

"Kenny!" Larry called.

"you want to conduct this operation over amateur air?" Froggy asked McKellar.

"you got a better suggestion?" he whispered back

"did you say there's a fire?" a young voice approached the phone on Larry's end.

"son, you said you wanted to serve your country," Larry said.

"uh... yessir?"

"you ready to do it?"

"... to put out a fire..?"

"are you ready, son, yes or no."

"well, yessir."

"even if it means the ultimate sacrifice?"

"Grampa, what's goin on?"

"even if it means--"

"yes, yeah, i'm ready."

"okay. well then get yer shoes on, and get the ham radio out of the den. we're takin it in the plane."

McKellar read from a pad Pepper held up. "Larry, tune to one five point three eight zero."

"fifteen three-eighty," Larry shouted. "got that, Kenny?"

"fifteen three-eighty!" he shouted back from another room.

"and where we goin?"

"head north," Howard said. "we'll give you specifics in the air."

Boyd stepped forward again. "Larry, this is a sensitive operation that we'll be conducting over open air. i think it best if we use code names."

"alrighty."

Boyd hesitated, then looked around the room, a sheepish grin betraying his calm professionalism. "i can't think of anything."

"i was always kind of partial to Roy Rogers," David said, shrugging.

"okay, Larry, we're Roy Rogers--"

"guess that makes us Trigger and Bullet," Larry said.

"perfect."

"all right, Roy Rogers. we're headed to lasso this sumbitch. talk to you in a few on fifteen point three-eighty."

"roger that, Trigger. over and out." and Boyd tossed the handset to Mo, who hung it up. "well." Boyd looked around at his men. everyone was standing. everyone was smiling. everyone had hope. even Mo. "yippee-ki-yay."

§

sleigh ride

David darted through the crowd of men toward the back wall of the cab. "comin through!" he ripped a map of Colorado Springs off the wall and shoved his way back through to the console. "show me where the salvage yard is."

Howard pointed. "here, near where the Academy's going up."

"okay," David said, drawing a near-perfect straight line indicating the rocket path. he began figuring angles, crunching numbers like a madman. adrenaline and hope electrified every thought. his pencil barely kept up. finally he drew a line from the salvage yard to the rocket path. "this is where they'll cross its path."

"that's right over Smith Creek out toward Monument. he can hit that no problem. just get him an altitude."

David scratched another formula. "i dunno how big a curtain he can give us, but this thing is coming through at about 1800 feet."

Boyd grabbed the map off the console. "we need to confirm that with the Denver tower. everyone downstairs!"

everyone parted ways as Boyd rushed down the stairs, map in hand. David and Howard followed. the rest of the men weren't far behind, and soon everyone was back on the floor.

"i hope they can make it that quick," Roberts said. "Fat Man detonated over Nagasaki at 1500 feet."

"1560," McKellar said. "it's gonna be close."

"just passed Denver," Burke said. "same heading and airspeed, 690 miles per hour."

"what's the altitude?"

"they read it at 5900 feet and descending."

David froze. "that's too high. why is it--"

"Denver's lower than us," Walter said.

David relaxed. "yes, thank you."

"so this is good?" the Colonel asked. "this is the plan?"

David held up a finger, doing the math in his head. "yes, sir. yes, we're right on. Smith Creek at 1800 feet."

Boyd leaned in. "they're in your hand, David. do you want to double-check--"

David looked dead at him. "Smith Creek. 1800 feet." Boyd nodded.

"come in, Roy!" Larry's voice fanfared from the PA.

"we read you, Trigger," McKellar said, back at his mic.

"i got the ACT-13 hooked into the ARC-5 so we can all talk to each other. got to load up the other stuff... standby."

David was looking at his watch. "they've got to get in the air."

"there's no point being in the air without the magnet and tow cable," Roberts said.

over the radio, the Avenger engine came to life. Pepper turned down the radio.

"you in, Bullet?"

"yessir!" came Kenny's young voice. Howard was frozen, eyes locked on the shortwave.

"okay, here we go."

the engine roared as the old plane sputtered and bounced along their dirt runway. the sound of glass breaking startled everyone.

"Trigger, what was that?"

"Roy, this is Bullet," Kenny said. "had to pop out my rear window to let the tow cable out. we're good."

the engine screamed as the prop pulled the heavy plane away from the earth.

"Trigger is in the air," Larry said.

"Trigger, you're going to drop this curtain over Smith Creek, covering the air at about 1800 feet. can you do that?"

the plane moaned and roared as they navigated take off and set off on course. "piece a cake," said Larry. the engine leveled out, still rising. "we're on course, Roy Rogers."

"Grampa, do i hang this out yet?" Kenny asked.

"no, hang on to it. we got drop our load first. get it wedged in there and then get on the bomb bay controls."

"yes sir."

"Roy, we got the wench on board, but didn't have time to hook it into anything. we got it wedged in pretty good with an inch-and-a-quarter iron pipe. i think that'll hold it."

Roberts shook his head. he whispered to Boyd. "six thousand pound glider against an inch and a quarter iron pipe?"

"we'll have to chance it," Boyd said. "unless you've got a suggestion."

he didn't.

"okay, Roy, we should be at Smith Creek in... oh, about a minute and a half i guess."

"we good on time, Michaels?" asked McKellar.

David looked at his watch. "it's close. they... really need to be going top speed."

"Bullet, you've got to be going top speed to make it in time," McKellar said.

"we got 'er wide open," Larry replied. "currently two hunerd and... seventy two m.p.h." McKellar looked at David. he nodded, tentative. "midnight ride on Christmas Eve! i feel a little like jolly old Saint Nick, fellas. course, you know why he was so jolly, dontcha?"

McKellar fought a grin. "why's that?"

"he knows where all the naughty girls live." a few of the men laughed. even Boyd and the Colonel. the humor sliced through the tension, and everyone relaxed a little.

except Howard. David realized, these are his friends. Kenny was probably about his age, maybe younger. David rested a hand on Howard's shoulder. Howard breathed slow and deep, his chin resting in the crook of his hand.

"now once i drop this pile, i gotta circle around out ahead of it, and we'll let the electromagnet out the back on the tow cable with the wench. i think we have enough electric cable to get it out past my tail."

"that's not running off a battery, is it?" Roberts asked.

McKellar relayed the question. "Trigger, is that on a battery?"

"the Avenger battery. as long as this prop is turnin, we'll have power."

"your pal Larry's a pretty sharp guy," Roberts said.

"so's Kenny," Howard said.

"you lucked out with the wind," Larry said.

"how's that, Trigger."

"calm as anything up here. won't have our spray floatin away." the engine purred hard. "Bullet! we're gonna get out in front of this glider, and you're gonna suck that magnet right onto to nose."

"yes sir, i'm ready."

"okay, comin up on Smith Creek. our altitude is a lil over 1900 feet, that will give it room to spread out and cover your window."

"Trigger, do you see the glider coming in?"

"uhh... not sure.. i see somethin out there, but could be a star..."

"ready with the bomb bay doors, Grampa!"

"okay, not yet, few more seconds. okay i see it. it's a ways away... jumpin all over the place?"

"that's it," McKellar confirmed.

"i need to be a smidge higher i think... get ready, Bullet!"

"i'm ready!"

"in 3... 2... 1... aaand now!"

metallic screeching preluded a loud jostling as the engine growled.

"damn! the drag on these doors bout to shake me out my britches."

"we're empty!"

"copy that, Bullet." the plane's roar curled into low groan as Roy brought it around. more screeching as Kenny levered the bomb bay doors shut again. "Roy, this is Trigger, the curtain is away. trying to get in line with this thing. wish i'd kept the radar, now. Bullet! i'm gonna get us close, but you're gonna have to guide me."

"hold on... letting the magnet out."

loud banging caused everyone to jump. "the hell you doin back there, son?"

"sorry, Grampa. magnet smackin into the tail."

"damage anything?"

"no sir! it's past it now.. about twenty feet past it, straight out behind us. the wind is too much, i can't control it... you're going to have to make contact by moving the plane!"

"well then you gotta be my eyes, boy."

"yes sir! hey, i see it! it's going through the manure! went right through the top of it! ha ha! almost missed it!"

everyone in the Command Center exhaled.

"that's step one," Boyd said.

"was there a flame out?" McKellar asked.

"not sure, Mister Roy.. it's comin up on us quick!"

"turn yer magnet on, boy!"

an electric hum created a layer of static on the radio. "it's on! higher! higher! it's gonna hit us!"

the Komet hissed past, no jet engine scream.

"went right under us!"

"i see it, it's out in front of us."

the men slumped. to come all this way, and miss the last catch.

"it's... gliding pretty good, but losing speed pretty quick.. gonna chase it... it's slowing down..."

the slumps slowly reversed themselves. Howard stood up. everyone was on edge.

"it's stopped getting away from us... it's pretty far out in front... but.. okay i think.. yeah, we're gainin on it now... boy kill that magnet!"

the hum disappeared from the transmission. "it's off!"

"now that the jet is dead, it's flyin straight as an arrow. easier'n ropin cattle. okay, boy, i'm gonna float right over the top of it. you watch it in your windows and help me lower it right onto it. when we got the magnet in the center of the nose, throw the switch."

"the nose is the warhead," Roberts said to Boyd.

Boyd turned to him. "isn't that the part we're trying to get rid of?"

"comin up on it, Roy! passin by under me, you see it, son?"

"looks like a shark! okay the tail is reaching the magnet.. up a little bit!" the engine gave a little rise. "okay... slow down, slow down more... okay magnet over the middle.. coming up toward the front... aaand..." the electric hum clicked into the air, followed by a thunk and jostling. and next, a loud holler. "whooooohooo! got it!"

"we got it?" Larry said, sounding surprised.

"we got it!"

the Command Center erupted. cheers and yelps all around. Howard didn't cheer. he appeared relieved. but it was a reminder to David... this wasn't done yet.

"remember not to let it get much lower," Roberts yelled over the celebration.

"Trigger, slowly pull up and head west!" McKellar said, smiling like he were flying that hot rod of a plane himself.

"roger that, Roy." the engine purred higher.

suddenly there was a loud commotion, and the sound of metal on metal. Kenny let out a loud scream.

"what was that??" McKellar shouted. Boyd quieted down the floor.

"Kenny!"

"i think i broke my leg!"

"what happened, boy?"

"this pipe snapped in half, that wench knocked me in the shin."

"Bullet, are you still towing the package?"

Kenny grunted, moving around the cramped quarters of the plane. "yeah, it's still there... the wench is wedged in the frame of the window... but... it looks like it's gonna hold."

"copy that," McKellar said.

"you bleedin, son?"

"i got a pretty good gash on my shin, but not too bad. i think i broke my shin bone though. hurts like the dickens."

"okay, we'll get it looked at, just hold on, son. hey Roy, how far we takin this thing."

"standby, Trigger." McKellar turned and looked at everyone else. "we got a plan here?"

§

with a tail as big as a kite

Roberts, Boyd, and David walked to the mapboard.

"are we just ditching in the desert?" Robert asked.

"i'd rather fly it to the Pacific and sink it as far out as we can take it," Boyd said.

"what's the range of an Avenger, somebody?" David asked.

"about a thousand miles." David looked to see the Colonel stepping up beside them.

"oh, thank you, sir. well..." David measured with his finger. i guess the shortest path would take them... here, between L.A. and San Diego."

"Airman, workup a flightplan, diverting them around major municipalities. and keep them at their current sea-level altitude or higher. i don't want this bomb going off when the ground drops out from under them."

"yes, sir. on it right now. Howard, you want to give me a hand?"

Howard stood, still staring at the radio. he turned, his eyes glassy. "uh, yeah." he strolled over to where David stood.

"hey, you all right?"

"are they gonna come home?"

"it's only about 860 miles to the coast. they should have enough fuel to drop the Komet in the Pacific and land somewhere in California."

Howard sighed. "okay." he cleared his throat as he surveyed the mapboards. "how can i help?"

the light atmosphere on the floor jolted to a halt when the black phone rang. the Colonel walked over to it and picked up the receiver.

General Partridge's voice came over the speaker. "Colonel?"

"yes?"

"you've made it through?"

"we have."

"i'm... glad to hear that."

"not as glad as i am, i assure you," the Colonel said coldly.

"well, that you're still there explains our good news. we had reports of bombers taking off from Soviet bases, but they've since turned back, every one of them."

"that is good news, General. you're welcome." the Colonel hung up the black handset. the men were stunned. Leonard laughed in disbelief, immediately covering his mouth. Mo clapped. the Colonel walked up to the first tier and poured himself a cup of punch and sat down, propping his feet up on the counter.

"he's gonna pay for that during the debrief," Roberts whispered to Boyd.

"yeah," Boyd said. "something tells me he doesn't give a shit."

over the next hour, the team worked together, gradually migrating back to their typical posts. David and Howard worked on a flight path, sending Larry and Kenny closer to the ocean, avoiding cities and towns. Marston, Burke, and Sollee were on the green phone checking with every tower, keeping the air space clear. they gave a cover story about some special radar equipment being transported.

the Colonel, Boyd, and the other brass resumed their spot up in the cab, discussing the cleanup. dozens of fighters — not to mention the three bombers — had been downed throughout the operation, and now there were some men out there on their own. they began crafting a cover story that it was a drill, war games. luckily, the three bombers all had U.S. markings, so there was little for anyone to suspect, even if they came upon the wreckage.

the trip to the Pacific was a four-hour flight in the Avenger. wind was low, and there was no turbulence, so Larry just puttered along toward the coast. Kenny was hurt, but had made himself as comfortable as possible. the airmen took turns at the radio with Pepper, mostly just keeping Larry and Kenny company. Larry was full of stories and jokes, and Kenny wasn't short on them either. everyone in earshot of the shortwave speaker was in a great mood.

Howard and David got the whole flightplan laid out on the mapboards and decided it was time for a break. Howard took over at the radio mic.

"Trigger and Bullet, come in."

"we read you, Roy."

"Trigger, this is your neighbor."

"Howard?" Kenny said. "what the hell'd you get us into?"

Howard chuckled. "sorry about your leg, Bullet."

"we'll shoot him when we get home," Larry said.

"hey... i know we can't say much, but... you guys saved the day big time tonight."

"so what is this thing anyway? is it Russian?"

"i can neither confirm nor deny," Howard said, smiling. "let's just call it a Komet."

"a comet, huh? you think they got a Donder and a Blitzen, too?"

"they might."

"they oughta call it a Rudolph."

"why, does it have a red nose?"

"yessir, commie warhead."

Howard chuckled, "hey Bullet, ixnay on the arheadway."

"right. sorry. hey, you wanna know the worst part about havin a broken leg?"

"what's that?"

"i'm gonna have a hard time kickin your ass when we get back on the ground."

Howard let out a full laugh, and a few others joined in. Pepper snickered with him.

just before 2300, Walter and Froggy brought the television from the break room and turned on the Christmas service from St. John's. they let the music and singing play for Larry and Kenny, but everyone else enjoyed it, too. David was glad to finally have some real church music playing in the Command Center.

midnight mass from Boys' Town in Nebraska came on channel 4 at a quarter til, and everyone gathered around the tv, even most of the brass. their shift was over at midnight, but no one was going anywhere until that package was away and Trigger and Bullet were back on the ground. third shift crew began arriving, and they were corralled into the conference room and served breakfast. the Colonel made the decision not to brief them on the situation for now, maybe ever. public perception of the U.S.'s strength versus the Soviet Union was a paramount concern, and it was decided the best course of action is if this quietly went away. David understood, but wished he didn't have to sit on a secret of this magnitude, quite possibly for the rest of his life.

following the midnight mass, Larry became rather sentimental. he and Kenny sang hymns, often forgetting the words. he didn't have much of a singing voice, but it was clear he meant every word. he really got into "I'll Fly Away" and "How Great Thou Art".

time passed. the flight was uneventful, and every time David thought about it, he thanked God. Larry was getting tired. not too tired to fly, but he was out of stories and jokes and didn't feel like singing any more. David offered to read some Scripture to him. he and Kenny both liked that idea, so David started in with some of his favorite passages. he asked them about some of their favorite stories from the Bible, and he read them to them — the parting of the Red Sea, David and Goliath, the conversion of Saul. he finally got to read a few proverbs, then, becoming tired himself, settled into the psalms. he started with psalm 1 and just read straight through, checking in with Larry every so often to make sure he was awake. Kenny had fallen asleep sometime during the march around Jericho, and Larry let him sleep.

eventually, most everyone was back on the Command Center floor, waiting to make sure the bomb made it safely out of the United States. as the Avenger neared the coast, Larry began to rouse, getting a second wind.

"so fellas." Larry's voice caused everyone to sit up. "we're getting close to the coast."

"another ten minutes or so," David said.

"yeah. so, what are we gonna do with this thing when we get there?"

David looked back at the brass, and McKellar stepped up. David gave him the chair.

"take it out in the water and drop it," McKellar said.

"just turn the magnet off and let it go," Larry said, looking for confirmation.

"that's it," McKellar said. "ideally, past the continental shelf."

"past the what?"

"it's where the land under the ocean drops off and the water gets very deep."

"and how far out is that?" McKellar looked at David.

David glanced back to the plexiglass chart. "about 180 miles past the coast."

"180 miles past the coast, Trigger."

a long silence on the radio.

"is this bomb live?" Larry asked.

McKellar was confused by the non sequitur. "there's no way of knowing, but we have to believe it is armed, yes."

"and it goes off... based on altitude?"

"we don't know, but there's a good chance it's set to detonate based on altitude, yes."

more silence as the radio crackled.

"what's the issue, Trigger."

"well. couple of things. for one, we'd prefer not to get our ass singed."

"copy that," McKellar said. "once you get out far enough, you could go high enough before you release it so you have time to escape the blast."

the radio crackled. everyone waited.

"no," Larry said. "we don't have the fuel for that. which is the other thing."

everyone sat up.

"you asked if we had a full tank, and i said yes, because it wasn't worth goin over the finer points at the time. we were close to full, but not full. and when the fuel runs out, this magnet is going to die and let loose mighty quick."

"okay, Trigger, so how's your fuel?" Boyd asked.

"i'm looking at... 120 miles. maybe a few more if i really stretch it out."

David walked to the mapboard and pushed his ruler up against the route. he counted and made a mark awfully close to shore. "that barely gets them past the coast," David said quietly to Boyd.

Boyd pointed to California's Catalina and San Clemente islands, just beyond David's mark. "they've got to make it out past the islands at least," Boyd whispered back.

"and they've got to make it back," Howard said, a desperation brewing.

Boyd looked him in the eye. "one thing at a time, airman."

David knew what that meant. so did Howard.

Boyd walked to the radio and took the mic from McKellar. "Trigger, we're going to need you to get every mile you can. if the package.. delivers.. the blast, the heat, the fallout is all going to come back onto the mainland. we want that to happen as far away as possible. again, ideally, past the continental shelf." Boyd looked over David's shoulder. "there's a Naval airstrip on the north end of San Clemente Island, right on the continental rim. you're going to pass it on your way out past the shelf. after you release the package, maybe you can make it back there to land."

David traced the route with his finger and added in his head. he looked at Boyd and shook his head. no way.

"how far," Larry asked, probably doing the same calculations in his head.

David measured. "from the coast, 66 miles to San Clemente, 170 to the shelf, at least."

Boyd relayed. "66 miles to the landing strip, another 90 past that to the shelf."

"then 90 back to land," Larry said.

they were still 25 miles from the coast. the arithmetic wasn't hard. it was on everyone's face. the silent radio drowned in it.

"Roy," Larry's voice, a hand piercing the surf, "can you read psalm 19 again?"

Boyd handed David the mic.

David took it, and spoke somberly. "absolutely."

the television was off. the turntable was off. the situation was tense again. not for the fate of the world, but for the fate of these heroes. every man in the CONAD Command Center owed his life to these two men. some of them had weighed enlisting for a long time before making the commitment. these two men had to make it in seconds, and they didn't hesitate.

David read psalm 19. and psalm 23. and psalm 46. they passed the coast. they passed San Clemente. David kept reading. no one knew for sure how much fuel they had left.

"did you see the sunrise this morning?" the voice on the radio was young and weak. it was Kenny.

"no," David said. "we were still asleep."

"i saw it," Larry said. "i had to fix a fence over at Judge Holder's."

"i didn't see it," Kenny said. "i was up."

a long silence.

"i didn't even look out the window," Kenny said.

"i saw it," Larry said. "but i didn't look at it." and he sighed.

it was midnight on the western coast, a long way from sunrise.

for the next ten minutes no one said a word.

the fluorescent ballasts hummed dimly overhead. the radio was staticky with the distance growing, the curvature of the earth rising between them. the electric hum of the magnet vibrated in everyone's joints. a radio squelch flashed through the room like a nuclear blast, and the men sat up.

"Roy Rogers, come in, this is Trigger and Bullet." the static was so thick, David could barely make them out.

"this is Roy, come in, Trigger and Bullet."

lots of static.

"hello?"

"Roy do you read us?"

David looked at Pepper, but there was nothing he could do. "we read you, Roy. do you have an update for us?" nothing. "would you like me to keep reading?" nothing but static. David pulled his Bible close. *"i cried unto The Lord with my voice; with my voice unto The Lord did i make my supplication. i poured out my complaint before Him; i shewed before Him my trouble. when my spirit was overwhelmed within me, then Thou knewest my path--"*

Boyd put a hand on his shoulder. "it's not getting through."

"it might be," David said. Boyd squeezed his shoulder. this was the end.

the static was getting worse.

"having a hard time hearing you," Larry's voice barely cut through. "guess we're at the edge of our range."

"we'll send a ship for you," David said. he looked at Boyd. Boyd frowned. it wasn't a lie. they'd send one. but the odds of a successful rescue were astronomical. David knew that. but he hoped. and he figured some hope might keep them aloft a little longer, if they could hear it.

"Roy, we're gonna sign off. send Buttermilk my love." the static was unbearable.

"yessir," David said.

"Trigger and Bullet, over and out." through almost pure static, his final words were barely heard: "happy trails."

§

midnight clear

the white noise of static blanketed the room in a harsh thicket. the men stared at the radio.

Boyd rose, straightened himself, took a deep breath, and raised a rigid hand to his brow, saluting the radio, where the brave men were last heard. slowly, each one in the room did the same. David released the tight grip his fingers held around the corners of his old Bible and stood. as he touched the tip of his finger to his temple, he hoped these men would be made honorary airmen in recognition of their commitment. after all, they'd made the sacrifice David had been willing to face when he signed on as an airman. they'd not endured basic training, or endless instruction, uniform and bunk checks, drills and exercises. but they'd been faced with the mission all servicemen fear — but accept — and it had cost them and their families all the same.

"God rest ye merry, gentlemen," Boyd said, and released his salute. slowly, the men relaxed. Boyd reached and turned off the radio speaker. the silence left a hollow ring in David's ears.

they stood at ease, statues. a full minute passed like a day, until a ringing broke the sacred silence.

it was the red phone. everyone stared up at it. David didn't hesitate. he walked straight up the stairs and sat down beside it. Boyd and Roberts walked up the stairs after him. he answered it, shaking.

"hello?"

"is this Santa?" the young voice whispered.

David unknotted. "this is one of Santa's helpers." everyone else breathed easier. David looked at his watch. "it's late. you should be in bed."

"i can't sleep."

the Colonel watched David. Boyd sat in a chair on the lower tier.

"you know Santa won't come until you're asleep," David said.

he could hear the shuffling of the young child on the other end. "i was afraid. i heard noises outside."

"you did, huh."

"in the sky."

"well. that might be Santa on his way to your house. have you been good this year?"

"uh huh."

"that's good. did you already tell Santa what you wanted?"

"no."

"hmm. well, i can send him a message if you like."

"i don't know what to ask for."

David straightened a wrinkle on his slacks.

"what would you ask for?" the little voice took David by surprise.

"i guess... i'd ask... for peace on earth. and to see the sunrise."

"all right. that's what i want, too."

"yeah? well. i happen to know for a fact, that Santa's helpers... have already given you that gift. it's headed your way. and they've given *everything* for you to have it. so, go get back in bed, little one. and don't be afraid. you don't have to be afraid. not tonight."

"all right. good night."

"good night."

"merry Christmas," sang the little voice.

David waited until the young child hung up, then he placed the receiver back in its cradle and breathed a sigh of relief.

it was well past midnight in Colorado Springs, and the skies were clear.

the Colonel turned and spoke to the men, using the stairs as a dais. "it's over. i remind you that each of you has strict orders not to talk about any of the events of this evening. outside of very specific, formal debriefings with me or Lieutenant Colonel Boyd, you may not even speak about it to the others who work here in the Command Center, not even to each other. not in the cubicles, not in the break room, not in the bathroom. is that understood?"

"yes, sir," every voice declared as one, echoing off the tiers.

Boyd stepped up beside the Colonel. "the new shift has been stuck down in the conference room for the last two hours, and they're getting a little stircrazy. no one says a word to them. they'll go about business as usual monitoring what they can. Mo and Pepper, brief them on the situation with the phones, and nothing else. everyone else, i know you've been here for your full shift and then some, but no one is leaving until we debrief each one of you. we'll call you in one by one, starting with Airman Burke."

"Bonner, you're gonna be right behind him," Roberts said, punching a serious glare his way. "bring that PA speaker with you." he went to the stairs, followed by the other brass.

Burke glanced at Mo, nervous. Mo stared at the floor. David worried what might happen to them. maybe they'd be given some grace. but grace wasn't something the military was particularly known for.

"Michaels," Boyd bellowed from the cab doorway. "box up your cubicle."

the blood emptied from his face. "... sir?"

"all post-event assessment, data gathering, and debriefing will be done in the cab. you'll be staying with us for a few weeks." and with that, the Colonel, Boyd, and every officer disappeared into the cab.

David breathed a sigh of relief and looked at Howard. Howard stood facing the wall, his chin on his chest. David gathered his things and walked toward the den, stopping when he reached Howard.

"i'm sorry about your friend," David said.

"yeah. me, too. proud as hell of him, though."

they stood together for a moment, quiet.

"Clarence."

"what?"

"Clarence," Howard repeated, "Clarence Todd. that's Larry's full name. and it's Kenneth Abernathy."

David nodded. "i'll make sure it's right in the reports."

Howard nodded a thanks. David patted Howard on the shoulder and headed to his cubicle.

David sorted through his manuals and binders, trying to remember what they already had upstairs. he debated over each binder before finally reminding himself he could just walk back down and get what he needed. he was moving upstairs, not overseas. he grabbed what he figured would be most pertinent and put it in his box, along with his pencils and slide ruler.

a body sneaked up behind him and set his open Bible on his cubicle desk. "might need this," Mo said.

"thanks."

David reached for the Bible, but Mo pressed it flat onto his desk. "i was... reading here. in Luke, where you left off before."

"okay."

Mo cleared his throat. his eyes were glassy and pink. "where they take the baby to this old man at the temple."

"Simeon."

"yeah. well. they take the baby to this Simeon and he tells them..." Mo squinted at the text, " ' Lord, now lettest Thou Thy servant depart in peace, according to Thy word: for mine eyes have seen Thy salvation, which Thou hast prepared before the face of all people; a light to lighten the Gentiles, and the glory of Thy people Israel.' and Joseph and his mother marvelled at those things which were spoken of Him. and Simeon blessed them, and said unto Mary his mother, behold, this child is set for the fall and rising again of many in Israel; and for a sign which shall be spoken against; (yea, a sword shall pierce through thy own soul also,) that the thoughts of many hearts may be revealed."

David looked at Mo. a tear beaded in the corner of one of Mo's eyes.

"this is... about Jesus?"

"yes."

Mo nodded. "i think tonight, the thoughts of my heart have been revealed."

David looked at him, praying for a response, but his mind was empty.

"you want to be like this Jesus," Mo said. he looked right at David. "and you are." Mo's voice was full of regret.

"Mo?" Walter's voice called out from the edge of the pit floor.

"yeah."

"they want you upstairs."

"well," Mo said to David. "time to 'depart in peace.' "

David stopped him with a hand on his arm. "you gonna be okay?"

Mo nodded, "personally, yes, after i sort some stuff out. career-wise? it was nice knowing you."

"maybe--"

"i... i can't be here. i can't handle... this. i couldn't do what those two farmers did."

"for what it's worth, i think you would have if you'd been in their shoes."

Mo forced a smile. "thanks, David."

Walter waited at the door. "Mo."

"coming." Mo took a deep breath, then followed Walter into the light.

David sat on the top tier, his box of supplies in his lap. debriefings were still going on in the cab, and he wasn't allowed in until they were done. he was exhausted, and his mind was coming off the adrenaline. his eyelids were finally starting to get heavy. it had only been about twelve hours, but it had felt like a week.

he looked at his watch. 0435. families would be waking up soon. children racing to the tree to see what Santa brought them. tearing into gift boxes for toys and sweaters from friends and family. firing up the oven for a Christmas roast. heading off to church in their Sunday best.

the Todd family would wake up to find two of theirs missing.

Majors McKellar and Tilday had been given the task of delivering the news to the family. they had to be exhausted as well. David imagined the burden of responsibility they had, having been awake for hours, instead of going home, going to deliver the worst news a family member could receive. and what could they say about it? they had locked themselves down in the conference room to get their details straight on the cover story. there wasn't one part of it that David envied.

he thought about Howard's friends and the great sadness they were about to experience. it felt so unjust. why is it evil attacks, and the good suffer. the men who commanded that bomber to destroy CONAD would sleep soundly and live to bomb again.

Larry and Kenny are not only dead, lost to the sea, but no one would ever know how magnanimous they had been for their fellow human beings.

"David."

he was startled to see Froggy suddenly standing over him. had he fallen asleep? surely for not more than a few seconds.

"Boyd's ready for you."

David carefully stepped into the cab, as if it were a precarious boat docked on a shallow shore.

Boyd sat alone at his desk, making notes. "you can set up in the corner, there, out of the way." he gestured with the back end of his pen, then went back to scrawling notes.

David sat his box down and carefully took his supplies out one at a time, like museum artifacts. he felt so out of place, an airman setting up shop in the cab.

Boyd slapped a folder shut and rose. with an armful of folders and papers, he walked briskly to David and pulled out a chair for each of them, like it was his own living room. David sat stiffly. Boyd sank into his chair and pulled an ankle up to his opposite knee.

"your performance tonight was exceptional, Airman Michaels."

"thank you, sir," David said, a courtesy.

"you disagree?"

"thinking about the casualties, sir."

Boyd nodded. "me, too. how about we remember the millions who slept without a care in the world because we are here."

David wanted to.

"what did you think you were signing up for, Michaels?"

"i wanted to protect the world from darkness."

"we all want that, to some degree. but we're only responsible for what's put in our hand."

"those farmers were in my hand."

"yes, airman. they were. i thank God they were."

David's eyes constricted, a gutter of sorrow welled up under them. "why? why wasn't there another way? why innocent civilians? why... why wasn't there another answer?"

"Michaels, if you left the safety of your home to face the darkness, you shouldn't be surprised to find yourself in the dark."

Boyd took the papers from the crook of his arm and held them out for David.

"everyone will want a full report. it will mean pushing your time off farther down the road. and you'll be locked away up here with me and Roberts for the next several weeks. but i need the help of a Senior Airman."

"Senior, sir?"

"i can recommend a handful of exceptional men for early promotion to E-4. your performance tonight earned it. given your first-hand participation in the activities tonight, not to mention your exceptional map-making and data gathering techniques, i'm sure the Generals will agree." he pushed the paperwork into his arms. "when they read the report."

"you want me to put together the report for the Generals, sir?"

"the Generals, other CONAD brass. SAC, the Pentagon, Joint Chiefs of Staff. the White House."

"the president?"

Boyd nodded. "your commander-in-chief." David stared at the stack, visibly apprehensive. "he's your superior, but he's just a man, David. just like you."

David held the materials, feeling their weight. "sir, i'm a farmboy from Kentucky. he's the leader of the free world."

"not tonight. tonight, the free world was in your hands."

David stepped out of the cab, floated down the stairs, lost in thought. he looked up to find himself on the pit floor. Howard was putting loose pages back into their binders. Howard looked up, and smiled when he saw him.

"i'm getting an early promotion."

Howard stood up straight. "oh."

"Senior Airman. maybe."

Howard smiled. "you deserve it."

David thanked him with a nod and shuffled for the exit.

§

repeat the sounding joy

David passed through the quiet lobby, now like a medieval chapel, dim flickering from fluorescents in the staircases, like the torch-lit wells of castle turrets, his footsteps' echo tarnishing the sacred silence. ahead of him, the glass panes invited the slow blue to greet him as, outside, the sun began to rise. the metal bar of the door was damp and warm and fogged around his fingers as he pushed, the thin skin on his knuckles slowly turning white.

he carefully stepped outside. there was no snow. it was cold and wet, and the air was heavy. everything was blue and sick. underwater. only Pike's Peak peered above the surf, the faraway sun beginning to reflect off its snowy cap.

David stopped halfway across the parking lot and turned to look at the Command Center. three windowless stories of stucco and cinderblock. the world could never guess what had just gone on inside. and no one would ever tell them.

David was silent.

he looked across the top of the Command Center into the northern sky, where death had been. the heavy sky was cloudless. or it was all cloud. no beginning, no end. it was too early to tell.

as the sun rose, wind pushed around the needles in the evergreens lining the lot. out ahead of him, a blackbird cawed, soaring in the distance. behind him, the chirping of a happy morning bird, likely sated by the wet worm of a winter day. beside him, the shuffling of an old chaplain.

"Yuletide greetings, friend."

David stared blankly at the empty northern sky. "hello."

the priest followed David's gaze into the nothing yonder, deep and blue. he turned to David and studied his face. "coming to chapel this morning?"

David turned to the old preacher. David's eyes were red from exhaustion and burden. "i'm not sure, sir."

"it's Christmas morning."

David remained stoic.

"the Child was born? King of the Universe? Savior of mankind?"

"yes, sir," David replied dryly.

"what are you thankful for, my son?"

David considered it. "peace on earth."

the concerned shepherd smiled softly at David, his eyes bright with the sparkle of a new day. "comes at a cost, doesn't it."

David didn't answer.

"the wise men brought expensive gifts from very far away. the shepherds left their flocks. the disciples left their boats. Christ himself left the security of Heaven, community with Father and Spirit, came to earth in pain and blood and scandal, and returned just the same. all for the hope of Peace."

David blinked, his eyes drying in the cold morning air.

"you young men. you've traded your lives for the hope of peace."

"will it ever come?"

the priest squinted into the sky where David stared. "...and i saw a new heaven and a new earth, for the first heaven and the first earth were passed away, and there was no more sea. and i saw the holy city coming down, prepared as a bride adorned for her husband. and i heard a great voice say, behold, the house of God is with men, and He will live with them, they shall be His. and God shall wipe away all the tears from their eyes; and there shall be no more death, neither sorrow, nor crying, neither shall there be any more pain: for the former things are passed away. and He that sat upon the throne said, 'behold--' "

"--behold, I make all things new," David spoke softly, his eyes an ocean. he looked at the wise old man. "until then?"

the old man's eyes smiled back at him, the universe was in them. they both stood silent. a chilled breeze bristled the cedars.

"well," the priest said, "until then, ...today is new. let's see what mercy it has in store for us." he patted David's shoulder, turned, and shuffled off toward the chapel. "merry Christmas."

"merry Christmas." David searched the vacant sky and waited on the sun.

§

about the author

paul andrew skidmore is a believer, follower, and filmmaker in Tennessee.

if you enjoyed this story, you might also enjoy a cup of coffee with its author. he'd likely enjoy it, too.

skidmorep.com/books
facebook.com/parabolosbooks
twitter.com/skidmorep